Dear Diary, Book Series

Book 2

I0565293

A Young Adult Novel

Dear Diary,
I'm Not Feeling Myself

By: Delicia B. Davis

Precise Publishing Group

Delicia B. Davis

Precise Publishing Group
New York

Copyright © 2019 by Precise Publishing Group

All rights reserved.
Precise Publishing Group:
233 Street Rosedale, NY 11422

Visit our website at www.ppgdreams.com

"Dear Diary, I'm Not Feeling Myself"
First Edition

ISBN-13: 978-0989225311

ISBN-10: 0989225313

Printed in the United States of America

"That's what I want to be, attractive from within.

Gorgeous for my heart and mind, not just for my skin…"

-Delicia B. Davis

UNLOCK YOUR SECRETS TO SET YOURSELF FREE

Dear Diary, Book Series

Dedication

❀   ❀   ❀

I dedicate this book not only to my students who I am committed to supporting in every step of their personal, creative, and academic growth; but also to the youth in my community who have experienced low self esteem, the absence of a loved one, or hate crimes used against them.

You are beautiful, inside and out.

My Inspiration

❉   ❉   ❉

As an avid reader in my youth, I also grew very passionate about writing. So at an early age, I began recording some of my deepest thoughts in a collection of diaries. This has always helped me to let out my pain, anger, fears, and joys when I couldn't contain them anymore. This story is a recollection of the experiences seen, heard, and sensed.

Although I've seen some challenging times, I learned to always persevere. You just never know how close you are to a breakthrough unless you *get through*. My encounters with hate have not only made me stronger but have forced me to grow. Through this story, I share with you my personal lessons in life and love. I truly hope the experiences portrayed in this fictional story evokes some **real** inspiration, strength, and change.

My Appreciation

❈ ❈ ❈

I cannot stress enough how much I appreciate the loved ones who supported me throughout the making of this book. Those who believed in my vision and continued to encourage- and even pushed- me to complete it. In my darkest of days when I was not physically or emotionally strong enough to continue on, I had such great motivators to help me through.

First, I give my thanks to **God**. I thank Him for my talents, my gifts, my creativity, my strength, my loving heart, and my sound mind. I thank Him for helping me turn every tragedy into a triumph and for allowing me to share the gift of love with so many others.

I would like to thank my sons, **Avery and Avion**, who have no idea how much of a role they play in my survival. Their smiles, their laughter and their love has given me reason to persevere daily. Times when I didn't even want to get out of bed were quickly negated by their heartfelt words such as, "Mommy, I love you", "You look beautiful", "Are you finishing your book?" and so many others. Their passion to grow as artists, dancers, athletes, and gentlemen have given me so much to look forward to in our present day and our futures. If ever I need a reason to accomplish a goal in my life, they give me two.

To my parents, **Delroy and Donna**, I thank you. Daddy and mommy set very high expectations for me to live up to. They encouraged me to do a lot with a little, and so I did. They allowed me to do more with my mind and less with materials. Because of that, I spent my entire life conjuring up creative thoughts, ideas, and visions. Most of all, they made me realize I had the power to bring them all to life. They've taught me to be strong in the midst of struggle, forgiving in the midst of pain, rich in the midst of squalor, independent in times of need, and faithful in times of doubt. Although I didn't always see the benefit of their tough loving actions, I definitely do now and want to thank them for giving me such beneficial gifts that will continue to radiate through me for a lifetime and beyond.

To my younger sister, **Dawn**, who is my confidant & very best friend, thank you for your ongoing love and support. You always have my back, support me in times of need and give me a helping hand in any way possible. Your maturity, spirituality, and strength have always inspired me. Even as the older sister, I look up to you, literally (lol). I will forever be grateful to you for being a sister, a supporter, and best of all- a friend.

To my only brother, **Delroy Jr.**, I've watched you grow up to be a smart, handsome, talented young fellow. I am proud to call myself your sister. When I lose all hope in the men of our generation, you continuously demonstrate what true chivalry, respect, and loyalty should be and most of all- that it still exists.

To my older sister, **Donel**, thank you for supporting my vision all the way through. You have always shared your gift of song and candid voice throughout my ever changing phases in this process. You've made yourself present for me; whether to swing by the house or to show up at an event, and that to me is priceless.

To my ever-growing extended **family**, I thank you all. As a parent myself, I know it takes a whole village to raise a child. So I thank all my aunts, uncles, cousins, grandparents, friends of family, adopted grandparents, God family, and loved ones who were instrumental in my life. I appreciate all times spent with you, learning, growing, experiencing, and enjoying life. These memories will never be forgotten.

To my **Precise Publishing Group** staff who have each helped build upon this dream with me, I thank and appreciate you. You each possess such profound creative gifts that have touched so many lives. As we enter schools, organizations, youth groups, media outlets, homes, churches, and more; I know I can trust you to deliver inspiration, motivation, and the vast creative skills that our company is built upon.

To my **friends**, I love you! I cannot express how much you each have touched and affected my life thus far. I appreciate having you in my life more than you'd ever know. I've spent countless nights out and many days in chatting, sharing, vacationing, dining, shopping, reflecting, experiencing, and living with you in my midst. I take my friendships very seriously so please know that anyone I call a friend, it is to my honor. Thank you for being there and answering every text, call, email, FB message, IG post, and more. Thanks for supporting my many events and limitless dreams. My life wouldn't be the same without you and I hope our friendship continues forever.

Diary Log

Delicia B. Davis

VOLUME 1: IT'S NOT ABOUT BEAUTY

Dear Diary,   *Monday May 19th*

I truly hate my body!

And would you believe the biggest party of the year just had to be at a pool- Kendrick's at that. He's the most popular guy in our school so it's not like I could just decline the invitation. Especially with my entire crew of friends expecting me to come along.

It pissed me off that I would have to be seen in a bathing suit by everyone who's anyone at Northfield High. So I have got to get my body right.

It just isn't fair though! Everyone doesn't have a perfect petite bikini bod. But my besties do and it really sucks for me.

I'm constantly compared to the awesome and amazing Tammy. She's the leader of our clique and rightfully so. She's beautiful, and talented, and also a great friend. But I'm so sick and tired of riding her coattails of perfection. There was no way I would ever measure up.

I was just a bit excited when I found out one of the girls in our crew, Tiffany who was even smaller than Tammy, is pregnant. I thought, finally someone else in the group would experience what it's like to be just a bit overweight for a change. Even if it was for the purpose of bringing in a new life and it was only temporary, at least for the next nine months, I wouldn't stand out as the biggest of the bunch. And a girl like me could use a break.

More than anything, it pissed me off that they let this new chick into our circle. Patricia was the worst thing that could've happened to me. She was more than petite. She was super slim, and worst of all, she was smart. For all our years of junior high school, it was just Tammy, Tiffany and I.

Tammy was the prettiest, Tiffany was the skinniest and I was the smartest. But here comes Patricia, desperately looking for a come up in the social world and she lands herself in my life. Just when I couldn't face another competitor, she weasels her way into our circle, creeps onto the cheerleading squad, missed half her classes this semester and still passes freshman year, then even finds her way on Tammy's good side.

So where do you think that leaves me? Back to being just the fat girl out of the group. I'm sick and tired of being labeled this way.

My hips are huge and sadly, my waist is it's match. Instead of having that snatched figure every girl wants- I have these child bearing hips that a girl like me certainly doesn't need. My cheeks are pinch-able, rosy and plump. My friends tell me it's cute but I know the truth, anyone would rather high cheekbones and a pointy nose than to have all this.

My nose is wide and round. My shoulders are broad and my chest sits a little too high up under my chin. The guys call me thick and give me all the wrong attention for it all. No matter what anyone tells me, I'm ready to make some serious changes.

I think I got it all figured out though. I already told my parents I want to get liposuction for my birthday and I know they can afford it. But my mother's talking about how I have to get into one of the Ivy League schools of her choice... So I'm guessing she thinks I can actually wait until I senior year to make these changes. *Forget that!*

I'll find another quick way to do this.

As for the pool party, I don't think wonders like this can happen quick enough. But believe me when I say, I will try everything I can.

Dear Diary,   *Saturday May 24ᵗʰ*

As I was woke up in my plush purple bedroom, my little sister was already up and looking through my closet for something to wear. I don't know what she was thinking trying to get my size 10 jeans to fit somewhere on her size 4 body.

She got my fathers genes I suppose. We were only 2 years apart but she was clearly never going to have the issues I was having with my weight.

But at the same time, it didn't seem she was worried. Daphne wore her clothes a little loose anyway. She didn't primp up her hair for school everyday like I did or accentuate her lean, athletic body with jewelry and fashion the way I urged her to. Her main focus was tennis so sneakers and cool match wear was the only thing she checked for.

I rolled over and faced her back as she ripped through my closet.

"Where's the other foot to these Jordan's?!" she insisted pulling out an old foot of my 22's.

"Daphne, leave me alone. It's too early on a Saturday to be pestering me for my stuff!" I exclaimed. "Don't you have sneakers of your own?"

"Everyone's seen all my kicks already. I need to rock something new..."

"Why do you care about having new sneakers all of a sudden?" I asked.

"It's a special match today. A co-ed match and I need to stand out. C'mon I know you know what's hot!" My sister wasn't giving up.

"Check my shoe bin, that's where I keep the old stuff," I said hoping she would finally get off my case.

"One sister's trash is another sister's treasure..." She happily searched through my bin. "Oh and I'll need a cute baggy top too."

"You know I don't do athletic wear, sis."

"Well whatever you have that's tight and skimpy on you will be loose and sporty on me. Now dish me the goods!"

I pointed toward the section of my walk through closet that had all the stretchy tops. I was a bit slighted by her comment about our size difference. Although I'm sure she meant not an ounce of malice, it still hurt.

She didn't have the same struggles I did. She wasn't as concerned with body image and social status like me. All she needed to do was win matches. So she was completely oblivious to the pain she just brought on.

I was envious of her ability to focus on skills and abilities more than anything else. I wish I could focus on achievements and things like that but in my world, winning meant beauty, fashion, and fitness. How did two sisters grow up in the same home just a few years apart and live in two different realities? I certainly couldn't tell you but I hoped I would see the light of hers someday.

I guess when you're blessed with other things you can win at and focus on, life is easier. But I wasn't exceptionally smart, or sporty, or skilled at anything. All I had was my image so I had to get it right.

My sister was still in my room, now digging through my accessories looking for something to pull her soft straight hair into a ponytail with.

"OMG! Come here," I gave up on letting her have a spree all up in my room. I took a scrunchie out of my own hair and offered to fix up hers with it. "I got you."

She sat down by my beside as I offered her a cute and sporty hairstyle she could rock today.

"How do I look?" She asked excitedly, posing in front of me. She looked amazing. I was so proud of my little sister for being more confident than I would ever be, and without even trying. "Gorgeous," I said.

"Thanks, sis!" She hugged me quickly and said, "But this is not about beauty. It's about being the best and kicking some butt!"

As she hurried out, her words remained. I shook my head, hardly believing my sister actually thought looks didn't matter. *How can anyone be or feel their best without looking it?* I thought.

It would hurt my head to understand that, so I just threw the covers over my head and went back to sleep.

CHAPTER 2: TOO MUCH BODY

Dear Diary,   *Sunday May 25*

"Wake up!" My mother was annoyingly shaking me to wake up for church today.

Ugh! is all I could think.

Every Sunday morning without fail, my mother would get herself showered and dressed for church and try to drag us all along. Thank goodness my dad wasn't with it so we usually had a choice whether or not to go.

This morning, I was feeling especially down in the dumps. I still hadn't figured out what I was gonna do about the pool party situation that was only 1 month away. I felt awful inside. SMH.

"Are you coming or not," my mother asked.

"Is dad going?" I asked, knowing he would be my way out.

"You know your father isn't going, but that doesn't have to stop you, honey."

"What about Daphne?" I asked. I hated having my mother go there by herself every week. I know her and dad were starting to really disconnect with each other lately and it wasn't a good look for her. Especially with all the judgmental folks are probably making their assumptions.

But if I was going to go, I needed to have company for when mom started hollering and catching the spirit.

"Daphne is beat after yesterday's match. She needs to rest up for school tomorrow," she replied.

Dang! Daphne always had a good excuse to stay home. I mean, athletes always do. And after missing her game to sleep in, I felt it was only right I got up and accompany my mother today. I didn't want people thinking she had no family or support. It's been weeks since any of us went.

At church, my mother seemed to be her happiest. It boggled my mind how she would conjure up the strength to get up every Sunday morning and be so joyful whether she was alone or not. It was inspirational though.

She and my dad were so different in that way. All he cared about was health and wealth and he played his role well. My mother was focused on making my sister and I skillful and spiritual. It was kind of cool having them both in my life. You get the best of both worlds I guess.

My mother's a homemaker- if that term still exists anyhow. She's the truest definition of it. Our 3 story home was well taken care of.

For as many years as I can remember, my mother has been out of work and in the home. She's taken care of our meals, takes us on countless outings, and attends all of our school functions and activities. She is always a shoulder to lean on in crisis and is active on several boards including the prestigious Northfield Civic Association, the neighborhood's elite organization for local residents to better this quaint little Long Island community. *As if it gets any better than this.*

So I guess you could say, life is good. Perfect in fact. But when I look in the mirror, all *I* ever see is flaw. No amount of money or prestige, family or friends could shake the pitiful feelings I felt about my weight.

And every year when springs and summers roll around, it gets worse. Everyone starts dropping off clothing, exposing beautiful body types, flat stomachs, and smooth legs-things I would never have.

Around here, soon as May rolls around it's the season of pool parties, beach days, and barbeques. I couldn't hate living in Northfield more for that.

I watched my mother dance and clap to the alluring sound of the spiritual music in the air. She is the most amazing woman I know. She's big boned like me but walks with confidence at all times.

I admired my mom for the way she loved herself and her family. I guess when you're married with children, there's no reason to sweat your size at all. You're just loved and you know it.

Well, I'll never get to the point of having a man- or even kids someday- unless I get my body on point from now. I just needed to start skipping meals and possibly even letting some meals I do eat, go. My parents would never approve of this so I'd have to do it on the sly.

With my mother as deeply involved in our day to day lives, I don't know how I'm going to pull it off though. But I had to make it happen or this upcoming pool party is going to be a huge embarrassment.

Dear Diary,   *Monday May 26*[th]

The girls and I went shopping afterschool today. We all had to pick out cute swimwear for Kendrick's party.

Tammy's driver picked each of us up from the front entrance of the school building. We discussed the latest tea while riding in the shiny black SUV to Northfield Mall.

"So what kind of swimsuit are you guys looking for?" Tammy asks us.

"I honestly don't think I wanna go," Patricia states.

That was great news to me. I hated having her around.

"Kendrick and I have had a horrible track record. I don't know what he'll pull out his sleeve of tricks next," she continued.

Patricia was referring to her freshman year hazing experience with Kendrick. He did everything from cheat on his girl, accuse Patricia of being the whore who seduced him, spread rumors about her being fast, and continued to use her for his own selfish pleasures. She quickly became victim to the most popular boy and star athlete at our school.

At the time, Patricia was new to the crew so none of us knew her well enough to care. But now, we had to watch her back. She was a part of the clique, annoyingly to me, and we couldn't have anyone disrespecting.

Tammy answers, "Girl, please. He knows not to mess with you anymore."

"Word," I jumped in. "We've known him for years and that's how he treats all the new girls he meets. You should be lucky he even noticed you..."

It was true. Kendrick only messes with good looking girls, petite girls. Needless to say, he's never tried to come at me.

"Besides, you're rocking with the best crew now," Tiffany adds. "And with me all belly outta shape, somebody else gotta represent in a two piece!"

I had no comment on the subject. I was always 'belly outta shape' and I sure wasn't gonna be rocking a bikini. The girls knew it too because they didn't even look my way.

"I'll pick up a bathing suit," Patricia said. "But I'll let you guys know about actually going."

We all shrugged. I couldn't care less if she went. She'd just be another skinny little thing on the pool deck making me look fat. I certainly didn't need that.

At the mall, my friends and I searched high and low for trendy swimsuits. Everyone found what they were looking for in the Victoria's Secret Pink store. But there was nothing in there to accommodate me.

"Damn, does every swimsuit have to be made of string?" I commented. It was exasperating searching and not finding what I needed.

"It's the Northfield way," said Tammy.

"What exactly are you looking for?" Tiffany asks.

"Something that doesn't expose all this junk I got in my trunk." I didn't want to mention my stomach that had gotten bigger since last summer.

"You should shop Vickie's swim collection online. They have a huge variety of goods there," Patricia suggests.

I rolled my eyes at her comment but knew she was right. I wouldn't find my size here in the Pink store. I'd have to order something unique to my size online.

"I doubt it'll get here on time, though. Maybe I'll browse a few other shops here while you guys go eat..." I was happy to separate from the girls, especially as they stuffed their skinny faces with fast food from the food arena.

"Sounds like a plan!" Tammy said. "Meet us by the Ice Cream Bar when you're done. All this shopping got me hot and drained."

I waved goodbye as they took off. *Whew*! I thought. Food and dessert would've been too much for me to watch my friends eat.

I headed to some of the shops I knew had clothes for more size-able girls. Shops my friends *never* had to step foot into.

After an hour or so, I found something I liked in Hot Topic. But I left there still determined to drop some pounds within the next few weeks.

Before meeting up with the others, I barfed up the breakfast I enjoyed with my family earlier this morning. I was happy to rid myself of those heavy waffles and eggs I ate. I successfully dismissed myself from lunch with the girls. *But how was I gonna get out of having dinner later when I got home?*

Dear Diary,   *Monday Evening May 26*

Being home released much of the anxiety I was feeling about the pool party. But as I was in my room perusing the internet for sexier plus size bathing suits online, I heard the voices in my parents room elevating.

At separate wings of the 2nd floor, it was rare for my sister and I to hear what was going on down there. I knew trouble was stirring.

I stepped out into the hallway and saw my sister's room door still closed. She often had headphones on when she was in her room working out or whatever, so she was oblivious to the noise.

As I walked closer to the room to eavesdrop, I heard their voices clearly.

"Why do you need to know my every move?" my father said.

"I'm your wife! The mother of your children. The keeper of this home! I have a right to know!" my mother exclaimed.

I heard the scuffling of a bag. *Were they fighting?* I couldn't tell.

"Evelyn, please don't go in there," my dad pleaded. My mother must've gotten her hands on whatever she was looking for.

"Why not? What are you hiding?" she asked.

"There are just some things a man would like to hold sacred," he said.

"If it's not of God, it isn't sacred, Manuel."

A true woman of God, my mother was right. I was so proud to hear her confronting whatever daddy was doing wrong. She was a woman of strength.

"Let me just explain," he said with a more mild temperament. "Put the iPad down."

"I won't put it down but you may explain," my mother said.

A brief moment of silence was followed by my fathers reply. "I have some new friends, Evelyn."

"New friends? Or younger friends?"

"Younger, yes. Just one or two."

"Two? Are they prettier, smarter, slimmer?"

"No ones more beautiful to me than you, E."

"So are they smarter or are they slimmer?" Silence followed. "What is it? Why isn't my friendship enough?!"

"Why do we have to go there, Evelyn? I love you and I love this family. Isn't that enough?" My dad said. "It's not like I'm leaving you for anyone. I'll always be here to handle my responsibilities."

This conversation was starting to confuse me. Why did my father need new friends? And if daddy wasn't leaving, why did my mother care? Was she actually feeling insecure because these friends could be women- prettier, smarter, slimmer women?

I never thought my mother would have been insecure enough to utter these words. But I damn sure was glad she did. If there was an inkling of distrust, she had to confront it.

Unfortunately, I was a witness to my parents' first sign of weakness. My dad was making new friends and if my mother didn't like it, neither did I. Certainly if she could put such angry energy into the issue, something was very wrong. But I no longer wanted to hear the bickering. I turned away and went back to my room.

I had to work out my own problems tonight.

VOLUME 3: KEEPING IT TIGHT

Dear Diary,   *Wednesday May 28ᵗʰ*

Daphne and I decided to hang out today. It isn't often that we have the same schedule or interests but I wanted to spill the tea about mom and dad's fight the other day. So I invited her to go rock climbing with me.

I figured I could kill two birds with one stone, spend some quality sister time and work out.

At the spot, we had a short wait time so we hung out in the food court chatting.

"How was the co-ed match, D?"

Daphne replied always full of energy, "Amazing! I didn't come in first but I placed. More importantly, the outfit you lent me did exactly what it was supposed to!"

"What's that?" I asked.

"It gave me some much needed attention from my opponents. The guys were so busy checking me and my team out, they couldn't perform at their maximum potential!"

"That's what's up," I gave her a high five. She was too cute. I was expecting her to say she snagged a great guy in the outfit I gave her but dudes were far from her mind. She was always focused on winning. And the attention she got from guys was pure strategic.

I thought about how unfair it was that she got the kind of attention she didn't want while I wanted it but could never get. *Smh*!

"Yea I know," she continues. "But we know it isn't fair."

"Don't feel too bad. I'm sure if the guys had a secret weapon they could use to distract you, they would," I advised.

"Very true."

"But anyhow," I wanted to switch topics. "Have you spoken to mom lately?"

"Uh yea, we all had breakfast together just yesterday."

"I mean, really spoken to her. Like, alone?"

"No, haven't had any time lately. My tennis season has really picked up so this is the first time I'm setting aside any time to really speak to anyone. Why?"

"Well, I heard her and dad arguing the other day and it didn't sound good."

"Maybe they had a bad day..." She suggested.

"No, it seems like more than that. They were really fighting."

"What's there to fight over, sis? Their life is perfect. Besides, things were fine at breakfast yesterday."

"Maybe from where you're sitting but from what I heard, their marriage is far from perfect."

"Whatever, I don't want to hear anymore about this. That's their business. I'm sure in just a matter of time, they'll get over it. And so should you," she suggested.

Maybe my sister was too young to understand. But I was thoroughly concerned. I witnessed my bestie Tammy go through a most tumultuous time when her parents got divorced. When her mother left the family to be with her yoga instructor, it broke her heart and her home. Tammy was never the same.

As strong and skilled as my friend is, nothing can replace the love you miss when a parent leaves the home. And although she seems good now, I know she's living in pain. I'm extremely protective of her for that reason. I know how much she needs us, the clique, because we are the family she lost.

I only hope Daphne and I never have to encounter that level of hurt. But even if we do, we know we'll always have each other.

Tammy didn't have siblings, and her dad became so engulfed in his work that she often missed out on time with him too.

Nonetheless, I respected my sister's wishes not to discuss my parent's business any longer. But I was the firsthand witness to the drama. So it was up to me to do something about it.

I know all too well how the lies and deception of a spouse could affect more than a marriage, but an entire family. I couldn't put mine through that. So I figured it was up to me to keep this family tight.

The rock climbing attendant called our name and Daphne jumped up with the quickness.

"Let's go!" She exclaimed.

She was way too excited. I guess fitness activities are to her what spa days are to me- relaxing. But this rock climbing thing was no leisure to me. I was here to get my muscles working so I can start a regular workout routine.

I'd recently done some research on the surgery I want to get and they recommended daily exercise prior to getting approved.

This was the obligatory beginning of my grand plan.

Today's sister day out was greatly needed for more reasons than one. I'd have to get my mother and father out sometime soon too.

Dear Diary,   *Wednesday May 28ᵗʰ Night*

Dinner was extremely awkward tonight. My father seemed to be overcompensating his wrongdoings with great manners and compliments. My mother was clearly upset but put on her best front as if everything was okay. My little sister was ignoring the signs of dysfunction. And I, was aware of it all.

"This is delicious!" Daphne exclaims.

"Well, your mother does turkey pot pie best!" My father added.

"As 'best' as a woman may be, some people will still go looking for better," my mother responded sarcastically.

My father looked up at her but didn't have a word to say.

I had to break the silence. "It gets no better than this mom! You're amazing! By the way, I appreciate you cooking lean for me and not sacrificing the flavor."

"You're welcome honey."

Daphne adds, "Word, if I were to give my team this recipe, they wouldn't eat anything else in life!"

"Go on and give it to them. I don't mind sharing," my mother offers. Her eyes shifted from my sister to my dad. "Food is one of the few things that are meant to be shared."

"Are new friends included in that, mom? Should we be sharing new friends?" I asked.

My parents looked at me startled. They questioned in their minds what I knew.

"Yes we should be. Especially with family, the people you love most. There should be no secrets. No lies. No withholding. Once we start keeping things from each other, we create a disconnect and no family needs that," she answered.

"I beg to differ, Evelyn," my dad cuts in. "When you consistently share so much, you start to feel as if nothing is yours. You start to feel trapped. You need some things that just belong to you. We are each our own people. We all need our own friends."

"That makes sense," Daphne says. "Me and Morgan could never have the same friends."

"But you would at least share your experiences with them with me, right?" I added.

"I guess so. If you care to know..."

"Well, that's what we mean," my mother said. "Those friends you have are not secrets. You would never lie to your sister about them. Matter of fact, the best part about having separate lives as sisters is coming together and sharing those encounters, right?"

"Most certainly," I concurred. "And if you ever feel trapped, I hope you'd come to me and talk about it." I directed my last statement at my sister but the message was truly for my dad. I didn't mean to interfere with my parents marriage but it had everything to do with me- with all of us.

I hoped and prayed they wouldn't fight tonight. I hoped they would just talk it through and work this little kink out.

VOLUME 4: FAMILY MATTERS

Dear Diary,   *Friday May 30th*

"Mom, dad!" I rushed into the house today. I was excited to let them know I'm taking them out tonight.

Tiffany's mother had gotten her the tickets to see *Cirque de Soliel* at Nassau Coliseum but she passed them onto me because she was feeling sick this morning.

I'd seen this show numerous times as a kid and it never gets old. It's gets more creative and entertaining every year, and it's always a unique experience depending on who I attend it with. This was a perfect opportunity to spend time with my parents and them with each other.

My dad was in the den, which had become more of an office space to him, when I rushed into the house. He was on the phone as usual and hushed me as I came in with all my excitement. So I moved on hoping to find my mother.

She was just coming in the house after me, arms filled with bags of groceries. "Hey mom, let me help you."

I took 2 bags out her hand and placed them down on our kitchen counter.

"So... What do you and dad have planned tonight?" I asked her joyfully.

"As you can see, I'm about to get dinner started. As for your father, I have no idea. Most likely working though."

"Can you guys *please* change your plans tonight? I've got tickets for Cirque de Soleil!"

"For tonight? That's awesome hon'. I'd love to go if the rest of the family can do without the feast I was about to lay down. But you know your father may have his own agenda, as usual..."

"Dad needs to put his family first for a change!" I said.

"Well if you can get him to," my mother replied, "I'm all for it."

I waited patiently at the door of the den with a little pouting and pleading.

My father finally agreed to come out with us to the show. He only required that my mother prepared dinner before we left.

She did as he said while he finished up some of his work and I got dressed. I was anxiously hoping my sister would walk through the door at any given point in time. But she never did. I was a bit resentful thinking about all the crucial moments my sister missed with the family. Similar to my dad and his work, it was as if she considered her sport more important than us.

I quickly shook the feeling out of my head though. I had to remind myself she was working toward a much bigger goal than I. Besides, tonight, my dad chose *us*.

The car ride to Nassau Coliseum, where the show was taking place, was smooth. My mother was clearly as excited as I was to be out of the house and out on the town. It wasn't often that we went out, just for leisure, and spent this type of quality time together.

My father was dressed in his usual work attire, a button down shirt and tie with perfectly creased slacks and shiny dress shoes. He didn't have a chance to change into anything more laid back and *Cirque de Soliel* appropriate.

On the other hand, my mother had taken a quick bite of dinner and spent as much time as she could getting dolled up for this outing.

Her hair was neat and her makeup was on fleek. It was a look my mother rarely portrayed. She put on a casual yet cute fitted dress that accentuated her wide hips and shoes that looked uncomfortable but certainly highlighted her shapely calves. I was impressed to see her stepping out this way. My parents looked great together and I was proud to be in both their company.

My mom was so focused on him throughout the ride. She smiled as they conversed and put her hands on him a few times. I tried to stay out of the business but I couldn't help but notice how he slowly turned from tense to tender as they reconnected emotionally as a couple. It was a mission I was happy to see accomplished.

When we arrived at Nassau Coliseum where the show was taking place, there were countless families rushing into the lobby of the arena. My dad grabbed my mother's hand and held her close. My mother grabbed mine.

We bypassed much of the crowd and went straight to our assigned gate, level with the main stage floor. I was excited to be there! It was hardly about the show either. It was about being out with my mom and dad, a rare opportunity for us all.

A feeling of pure bliss came over me as I sat down beside my mother and looked up at both my parents. My dad put his arm around her and put one foot up on his knee. He was comfortable which made my mother exhale with ease. She seemed happy, moreover fulfilled in that moment. I wished for nothing more than this moment of comfort to last forever.

When the lights dimmed, however, my dad got a call. He glanced at his phone, took his arm off my mother, and was anxiously sending a response. She tried to remain oblivious to his new focus but couldn't help the side eye and a nudge.

"Sorry hon', I have to take this. Be right back," he said. "Y'all need a snack or anything?"

"I'll come with you!" I said excitedly. "I could use a drink."

"No, you'll miss the opening," my dad insisted. "I'll get you guys a water."

A water? I thought to myself. *Was my dad trying to insult us? What if I wanted a Coke? Maybe he doesn't want me gaining anymore weight.* Smh.

My mother must have shared my thoughts as she looked at father's back hurriedly moving away and then at me. She just shrugged her shoulders. She was an amazingly strong woman and would not want to show me any signs of insecurity, especially in public. I averted my attention back to the main stage of the arena. The show was beginning and my dad was no where to be found.

My dad taking as long as he did getting back was clearly making my mother uneasy. She turned around several times awaiting his return but he was no where to be seen.

As the show began, my mother was unable to focus and enjoy it.

"I'm going to the bathroom," I whispered to her.

"You're gonna miss the opening," she replied.

"I'll catch on."

"Let me come with you," mom said.

"No, daddy will be back in a moment and will worry."

She agreed to remain seated as I perused through the arena in search of my dad. Of course I went to the bathroom first, just to clear my conscious of any perception that I'd lied to my mother.

As I continued my quest to locate my dad, it didn't take long for me to find him by the condiments counter chatting with a young, beautiful, slim woman.

This must have been what my parents were arguing about the other night! I thought. I stood back in shock, watching my dad smile at and charm this woman as she handed him a card, possibly with her name and number on it. They exchanged a few more words and just before they parted ways, my father snuck a kiss on this woman's cheek.

Ugh! I was disgusted by this whole ordeal. I was seeing a side of my father that I never knew him to have. My feet were locked in place as I tried to make sense of what had just happened in front of me.

My father finally turned to walk back into the arena, with a full smile on his face. He noticed me, frozen in place and quickly changed his whole demeanor.

"Hey honey, did you want something to eat with this bottle of water? Anything?" he offered me.

I was still in shock and could not respond. "Let's get you some fruit snacks and a hot dog. You mother must be hungry by now, too," he continued.

So we went to the snack counter and purchased some food.

"Thanks dad," I said. And that was the only thing I could say to him all evening.

Dear Diary,   *Saturday May 31ˢᵗ*

Back at home, I lay out on my bed exhausted and uneasy. I couldn't stop thinking about the future of my mom and dad.

I felt awful keeping it to myself that my father had a private encounter with a woman while we were all out as a family. Just a few hundred feet from my mother who was grateful to be out as a trio, my father stood there and entertained another woman right before my very eyes.

As much as he thought he had betrayed *her*, in my heart he betrayed me too. And me not saying anything and simply returning to our seats as if everything was normal- made me a liar too.

I felt awful about the whole ordeal. Smh! I knew from now on, I could never agree to go out with my parents in such a way. Not without my sister, at least. Daphne would have known how to handle this much better than me. She would have either brushed it off as a mere casual encounter or called dad out for his behavior. Either of which would have been better than my reaction- disbelief and cowardliness.

As I watched my parents interact as friends and lovers for the rest of the night, I grew utterly confused. I reminisced on how my father held my mothers hand and gently rubbed her back as we walked back in the house tonight. He whispered something in her ear then kissed her neck as they left me in the kitchen only moments earlier. He acted as if there was no other. And in that moment, I no longer understood love nor the truth.

Dear Diary,   *Sunday June 1st*

I grew hatred for myself overnight. I couldn't forgive myself for allowing my mother to believe my dad was an honest man. I wanted so badly to rush into their room and distract whatever acts of love they were expressing to each other. I started to feel responsible for his dishonesty.

Halfway through the night, I got up to go to the bathroom and wash up.

When I looked into the mirror, it all made sense to me. My overweight image and that of my mothers- was totally to blame.

No man wants a woman who gained as much weight as she had since they met. Not when there were skinny Minnie's walking around town giving it up.

It was no wonder he kept his eyes open for his next come up. He was probably not attracted to her and disappointed in the changes to her image.

I've seen their old pictures. And while my mother has always been a beautiful woman with an amazing heart and soul- a man needs much more than that I'm sure. He probably desired the sexiness my mother once had long ago. *And the nerve of him to have such desires!*

My mind went racing. I couldn't erase the speculative thoughts of my father doing something to betray my mom. I couldn't escape the awful thought of my mother letting him bring her any pain. I tried so hard to shake the feeling but it wouldn't go away.

I couldn't sleep tonight. I cared too much about my parents and their personal ordeals. Surely Daphne wouldn't approve of me over processing tonight's events, but I felt I had every right.

As I pondered what to do, I went into the kitchen and the remembered the pralines and cream ice cream that was left in the freezer. Filling my stomach with such decadence was much needed to calm the anxious frustration I was feeling.

With every taste I savored, I felt a bit more hopeful. Every bit of deliciousness helped rid me of the bitterness that sat on my heart this evening. For several moments, I couldn't care what my mom and dad had going on. It was none of my business. For the decades they'd been together, I assured myself they would work this out.

My mother is a fighter and would never let anything or anyone come between her family. I was tripping to forget that our family is unbreakable. I felt a bit more calm.

Before long, I realized I had finished the entire tub of ice cream. Not feeling quite satisfied enough, I licked the brim of the container and then sucked on my spoon.

When I saw there was nothing left to delight myself in, I was overwhelmed with sadness again. Not only had I been helpless to my parents, but I packed on way too many carbs and calories within a few minutes time. I felt worthless and dumb.

It was my fault I was overweight. I have no self control. I pretend to eat my troubles away but know they're still there. It's even my fault dad even had the opportunity to kick it to that woman tonight. I brought him out and allowed him to stray from us. After all, he was getting me something to drink. *Shame on me!*

As I lowered my head with regret, I was interrupted by the sound of the door.

"What are you doing in here sitting in the dark?" Daphne said, turning on the kitchen light. She had her tennis bag on her shoulder and book bag on her back. It must have been a long day for her.

"Having a midnight snack," I replied. "What are you doing coming home so late?"

"You know the drill, sis. After school tutoring, tennis practice, and the gym. And of course I had to eat after all that..."

"Yea, yea," I got up to dispose of the ice cream container before my sister took notice of how much I ate. "With all that practice, you're missing out on a lot around here Daphne."

She goes into the fridge for a water bottle. "What? A little broadway show today and maybe a movie night tomorrow? Look, I got big dreams Morgan. I can't be sitting around entertaining other people's."

"Whatever D," I couldn't understand her disinterest in our personal lives and she didn't understand my interest. "I was referring to our time together- a little quality time. But I'm sure since it's irrelevant to your tennis championship, it's irrelevant to you."

Daphne sits beside me at the island counter. "That's not what I meant, sis. I just don't have time for leisure activities."

"So you don't have time for us now?"

"It's the high point of season. Championships are coming up. You know how much that means to me."

"S-M-H! So we don't matter no more?"

"C'mon Morgan. You know this family matters the most to me. And y'all know how much tennis matters to me. So I hope you can just support me in this and not punish me for having ambition."

She was right. I should be more supportive to her. She was the youngest and was the most goal oriented of the two of us. So it was on me alone to keep us tight.

I replied, "You're right Daphne, and I do support you. You know that. I just miss you sometimes. Days go by without me seeing or talking to you. And this family is all I have to lean on. It's just hard for me to understand how you could move like that..."

"It might not make sense to you but it's the only choice I have, sis. I have to keep my eyes on the prize at all times. TV shows and petty gossip do not fit into my game plan. The day I rest and relax, I lose stamina, I gain weight, I move slower, and I lose a match because someone out there got a day more practice than I did. I'm sorry if you don't get that. But one day when you figure out your ultimate goal, you won't let anyone steer you away from the finish line either. Trust that."

Dang, my little sister had her head on straight! I hated how right she was and how simple she made it all seem.

I did have an "ultimate goal"- losing this darn weight! But it was easier thought of than done for me. Although I know it seemed easy enough to just cut down my eating, exercise, and drink water; none of these activities were going to satisfy my daily desires.

My insecurities taunt me day in and day out which drives me to eat, which makes me weak, and water alone will never fill the emptiness I begin to feel.

All I could say to my sister though, was, "You're probably right." After that speech, I couldn't force my problems, or that of my parents, on her. I needed her to focus and win.

Instead of wallowing in my guilt and self pity any longer, I readied myself for bed. I'm pretty sure the clique would love to hear the latest on my family drama when I see them tomorrow. So I spared my sister the details of tonight's events and went off to sleep.

I tossed and turned a bit as my mind was filled with thoughts of my family's disconnect and my body's deterioration. With no one else to talk to, I was anxious to vent to the girls later- not that they'd understand but at least they'd listen.

VOLUME 5: THE END IS NEAR

Dear Diary,   *Monday June 2nd*

Patricia and I were the first ones to meet up in the cafeteria during lunch today. It wasn't often that I spent any exclusive time with her. I hated her guts but still, I couldn't help but respect her.

We all knew Patricia had been through a lot this year. The things she'd encountered at school alone was enough to make any teenage girl want to throw in the towel of life.

Within our first year of high school, we'd witnessed her getting rejected from the cheerleading squad, threatened in the locker room by an upperclassman, get taken advantage of by several of the most popular guys we know, and damn near getting kicked out of school for all the cutting she did to escape the madness.

Only because of the personal trauma she reported at home- abuse, suicide, assault, the attempted murder of her boyfriend, finding her father in prison, and being displaced from her home- she was excused for her absences and granted extensions on all her assignments. It was a wonder to me how she could even be standing here in front of me with a smile plastered on her face. The girl had strength.

"Hey, Morgan," she greeted me with our crew's exclusive hand motion. "I think it's just you and I today. Tiffany wasn't feeling good today so she's at the doctor. And Tammy is meeting up with one of her teachers."

Just great, I thought. *If I knew the other girls weren't coming along, I wouldn't have been here either.*

"Well, whatever," I started unwrapping my burger. "So what's up?" Maybe this was my opportunity to get to know her better. Not that we would find anything in common with each other but at least I'd try.

"Nothing much, I'm hanging in there as usual..." she lowered her head and went in her paper bag for a turkey sandwich.

"Yes, I see that. You always keeping your head up, girl. Don't stop now," I encouraged. "Seeing you make it through the hardships gives me the hope I need."

"Really? I never thought of myself giving anyone hope. Nor would I think any of you girls need it..."

"Well I can't speak for anyone else but I know *I* could always use a little hope. Times get tough for everyone at some point in time."

"Care to share..?" she asked.

I looked up at her. She showed genuine concern in her eyes. But I could not be vulnerable with her. There was no way in hell she would ever understand my troubles.

"Not really, you could never relate," I replied.

"Well, I'm here for you Morgan. You know pretty much all my business- I guess the whole freshman class knows- but you and the girls haven't judged me or abandoned me through it all. I want to give you the same loyalty, if you'd let me."

She was right. Although I wasn't fond of the girl- she was down for the crew. She understood the importance of trust and loyalty so I really had nothing to lose here. Besides, I really needed to vent.

"Okay," I cleared my throat to speak. "Have you ever felt self conscious? Like you're losing control of your life?"

"Wow, *have I*? Girl, that's how I've felt most of my life!" Patricia's statement gave me a feeling of relief. Maybe this phase I'm in was normal. "But I recently learned that none of that is true. We are always in control of our lives. And the only time we lose it, is the time we give it away."

"What do you mean?" I asked. "There are plenty things we have no control over and never will."

"Our lives aren't one of them, hon'. Just because we can't control other people, doesn't mean we have no power."

"How can you say that?" I asked puzzled. Maybe the girl *was* nuts. "Sorry to bring this up but when your mother was beating on you all those years, what power did you have then?"

"I'm glad you brought that up... To be honest, I had the power to tell someone, anyone. But I allowed her make me think I had no way out which is why I never went looking for one."

"Okay, I got you." I couldn't believe she was schoolin' me right now. Patricia was a lot stronger than she looked.

"You look like there's seriously something on your mind," she looked at me truly concerned. "I been through it all, girl. Tell me what's up Morgan."

"I'm just not feeling it these days..."

"Like how?" Patricia asked.

"Not feeling my body. Not feeling my looks. Not feeling my*self*." Damn, I just let it *all* out.

"Wow, that's no good."

I rolled my eyes, "Duh, I know that... Which is why I shouldn't have told you." I gathered the trash from my lunch and got up to leave.

Patricia put her hand on my shoulder. "Please wait. I meant, it sounds like you're a little depressed."

31

"Oh gee, thanks. Now I'm a sicko."

"No," she said. "You're just as normal as everyone else in the room. We all feel like that sometimes. But not everyone does anything about it."

"Well, there's nothing I can do."

"That's not true. You told me which is more than enough. Now I'm gonna make sure you get through this alright."

"How you gonna do that? You gonna be my chaperone or something?"

"Whatever you need from me, girl. When I'm feeling all sad and alone, all I need is a friend. If I can save you from that feeling just by being by your side, I'll do it."

"Yeah?" I questioned. "Well, that won't be necessary. Thanks though." I got up again to leave.

"But you didn't explain what's making you feel this way..." I heard Patricia say as I walked away. I'm glad I didn't get into the details of why I felt this way. I had said way too much already. Besides, there was no way in hell she'd understand my weight issues or that of my home. She didn't have parents nor siblings in her life, so sharing my troubles would be going way over her head.

I'll just wait around until Tammy, Tiffany, or my sister had some time for me. They would surely understand me better than anyone could.

Dear Diary,   *Thursday June 5ᵗʰ*

It was almost the end of the week and I had not yet gotten a moment to speak to Tammy, Tiffany, or Daphne about the things that were tugging at my mind.

I couldn't focus in class today, even as my teacher announced dates for our upcoming finals. I recall writing them down but definitely didn't commit any of the information to my memory.

I was busy doodling in my notebook, drawing sketches of myself as I wished I could be. In my perfect world, I'd have a slim waist and a flat stomach. I'd be beautiful, with pretty eyes, deep dimples, and brown hair. I'd be the object of every guys affection. I'd have to swear off all the hottest dudes in our class and save myself for someone special- the one I noticed when I passed by the school's fitness center last week- Troy.

Yes, he's an upperclassmen- only a sophomore though. He's slightly big-boned and has been in the gym everyday. I hear he's trying out for the junior football league next semester. Yea, I found out his schedule too so I've been checking him out regularly- stalking him even. And to no surprise, he still doesn't know I exist.

I thought back to what Patricia said about taking control. I needed to exercise my controls with him and fast. Once the other girls noticed his bodily transformation, I would stand even less of a chance. Especially if he made it on the league, his standards would raise up a few more notches and I would never be considered.

Too bad I didn't have the confidence to approach him. My body was in no shape to be flaunting around my crush anyhow. With Troy now within my arms reach and only a few more weeks until the pool party, I needed to take action or I go another summer fat, single, and sloppy.

I promised myself a change with whatever power I could conjure up. I needed this to be the kind of change everyone would see.

Dear Diary,　　　　*Saturday June 7th*

I decided to take Patricia up on her offer to help me through this awful ordeal I'm experiencing.

I called her first thing this morning because I needed her to motivate my new workout initiatives. She was already up and about getting ready to visit her boyfriend at the hospital. When she said she could help me if I make that quick stop with her, I agreed.

She and her temporary guardian, Dr. Graham, pulled up in front of my house within an hour of us speaking. I respectfully greeted them both as I got in.

"I was surprised you called me," Patricia commented when we were all settled in. "Heck, I was shocked that you were even up so early on a Saturday!"

"You and my parents both," I joked.

"Meet Dr. Graham, she's the one I'm staying with while my mother gets better," Patricia introduced.

"Oh, cool. Thanks for coming for me. I really needed a day out of the house."

"I know how it could be," Dr. Graham answered. "Teenagers do have it rough!"

"We do!" Patricia laughed. We all knew she'd experienced the most tumultuous past year than anyone else.

We both laughed in agreement.

"So, what kind of doctor are you?" I asked Dr. Graham.

"Great question," she replied. "I'm a psychologist. A doctor of the mind."

"So you do brain surgery and all that," I responded. "Yuck!"

The doctor chuckled. "No, not at all. That's a different kind of doctor. I study the mental state of an individual. I heal the mind from an external standpoint. I don't go inside the brain to do so, either. I can do it just by speaking with someone, observing their behaviors, and monitoring their emotional state."

"Yeah," Patricia added. "Dr. Graham helped me a great deal with what I had going on this past year."

"How so?"

"Well," Patricia continued. "She allowed me to express myself openly and without judgment. She asked me the tough questions I never wanted to ask myself. She helped me realize I was not the cause of my problems but I was an enabler of them. With her help, I gained the power to stand up for myself and realize that the end of my painful days were near."

"Well, dammit! Can I get a dose of that!"

Patricia had gotten involved with a guy she met in the streets during a painfully lonely time living with her mother. This boyfriend of hers, Diesel, was her escape from the madness. Turned out, he had a heap of hardships of his own. And today, Diesel is laying in a hospital bed fighting for his life after being randomly shot on the corner of his own block.

It was a wonder to me how Patricia could be so hopeful for her man. He put her through so much already- physically, mentally, and emotionally- and here she was, still running to be by his side. Dr. Graham must be very good at her what she does to have pulled Patricia out of that rut.

After a pretty quick ride to the hospital, we waited an eternity to be allowed in his room. While inside, it felt like hours before Diesel woke up. He had been in a coma for weeks and only recently had Patricia been alerted that he was awake and could receive visitors.

He wakes up and struggled to say, "Patricia... I don't think I can fight anymore."

"You need to fight, Diesel," she responds.

"What does my life even matter?" Diesel questions.

"It matters to me, babe. It matters to us. You know that."

"Oh my gee!" I interrupted. "I'd say get a room, guys, but I see we're in one! So I'm gonna leave you two lovebirds in it alone!"

Patricia chuckled a bit. "Sorry Morgan! Thanks for coming with me though. Couldn't have waited as long as I did without you."

"No doubt, Patricia. I'm glad I came." I gave Patricia a hug then turned toward Diesel to offer a few genuine words before walking out the door. "And Diesel, I'm glad you made it. Now, you better not leave my girl alone again."

As I walked out, I caught one more glimpse of the passion Patricia and Diesel shared in that moment. He took her hand and smiled.

As she leaned over his bed with eyes fixated on his and hands interlocked, I grew envious. I wanted to experience that kind of affection for myself.

I decided in that moment, that I had to experience my own version of love. Someday, some way, I needed to know what it was all about.

Dear Diary,   *Sunday June 8th*

As I stared into my full length mirror back at home this evening, I hated what I saw. I stood before my naked reflection assessing myself for anything other than a flaw. *Was my mirror broken?*

My image was sloppy and out of shape. Even sucking in my stomach and extending my torso wouldn't fix the overarching issue. I had to lose weight and do so, quick!

I wish even one of friends knew what it was like to feel so ashamed of themselves. Then maybe I'd have someone to share these painful thoughts with. Someone who didn't make me feel like a huge whale every time I stood beside them.

I shook my head one last time before throwing myself into bed. It was too early to be sleeping but I slept heavy to make sure I'd miss dinner tonight.

With all my recent dieting tactics, the end of this torturous image is hopefully near.

VOLUME 6: TAKE MY BODY

Dear Diary,   *Monday June 9ᵗʰ*

I got dressed today in some of the most appealing clothes I owned. After checking YouTube for some quick tips to appear slimmer, I decided to wear a black v-neck sweater top with some black and white patterned leggings. I straightened out my hair and wore a headband with sparkly cat ears. Then, I highlighted my lips with colored lip gloss.

I felt beautiful after adding all these beauty extras. But when I slid my hand on my hips, I knew what awful reality still existed. I was more than just a thick chick. I felt fat.

I only hoped that Troy wouldn't judge me by my cover. Maybe just maybe, he would see my heart.

I was so busy daydreaming about the end of the school day when I'd begin to stalk Troy in the weight room, that I didn't notice my science teacher plop a C+ on my desk.

Ugh! I thought. I needed at least an B+ to pick up my average before the end of the school year. I didn't want anything standing in the way of me receiving the ultimate birthday gift I'd been asking my parents for.

Maybe if I spoke to my teacher about extra credit, he may grant it.

"Mr. Granger? Can I speak with you?"

"Yes, Morgan. What can I do for you?" He answered. "You didn't seem so concerned with my class just a moment ago."

"I know. I'm sorry, sir. I've had a lot on my mind," I said hoping to be excused.

"We all do. Here in school, you can let go of all the things you can't control and focus on the things you can. Like your grades," he replied.

"Yea... Thats what I wanted to talk to you about. I have been trying my hardest to get my grades up and this C+ isn't good enough at this point."

"My thoughts exactly, Ms. Sawyer. What are you going to do about it?"

He was not going to make this easy for me. "I was thinking about doing some extra credit."

"I'm not offering any extra credit at this point. There are only a few days left for me to enter grades," he said sternly.

"Mr. Granger, I really need to bring my grades up before the year ends. Or this could ruin my summer- my entire life even!" I begged.

Mr. Granger pondered to himself for a moment. He looked inside his grade book then returned his attention back to me.

"Alright Morgan. If you can present a lesson to the class on one of the human body systems we covered this past quarter, I will add that grade to your final average," he offered.

"Present? A whole lesson? In front of the class?" I repeated. I hated even raising my hand and speaking amongst my peers. And here my teacher was asking me to present an entire lesson on something I had no idea about?! I shook my head in defeat. I doubt I could pull this off.

"And I'm expecting to have this assignment completed immediately following the weekend," he finished.

I remained in the classroom stunned by the details of this assignment. So many things crossed my mind. None of which had anything to do with the scientific content.

What would I wear? How would I look? Would my classmates make fun of me up there? Would I sound like a dummy?

I'm much more used to performing with a group like when I cheerlead. Dancing is something I love, nothing like public speaking. This would be totally different than performing. It was another opportunity for me to be humiliated.

I left the room much more disappointed than I'd walked in. I didn't have the confidence to go after Troy the way I had planned. Today, I had to focus on getting this assignment ready in just a few days. I couldn't even meet up with my friends. I felt like a loser for even needing to do extra credit. And for needing to prove to my parents that I deserve this weight loss operation. Why did I have to get the chubby genes anyway? *Life just sucked.*

Dear Diary,   *Tuesday June 10th*

Just when I thought things had gotten tough enough, cheerleading practice was a drag today.

Our captains began teaching us new chants that we should consider practicing throughout the summer in preparation for the upcoming school year. I was struggling a bit when one of the co-captains pulled me aside.

"What's the matter, Morgan? You can't jump any higher than that?" she asked.

She must have picked up on how challenging this new chant was for me.

"Sure I can, it'll just take me a little more practice," I replied.

"We may not have the kind of time you need to get yourself together."

"What do you mean?" I asked, continuing to practice.

"I mean, you've gained a lot of weight this year. Who knew your freshman fifteen would strike you in high school," she laughed. "And you know what that means..."

I kind of had an idea. "No, not exactly."

"It means, if you continue gaining through the summer, you wont be able to fit into your uniform sophomore year. And in that case, you won't be performing with us."

It was my greatest fear of all. This awful weight issue of mine could cost everything I lived for- cheerleading and performance. It could cost me my popularity and my friends. *Who would replace me on the squad? Patricia. Or even worse, an incoming freshman?*

"Don't you worry, I'll have my weight under control this summer. I'll be in even better shape than when you met me, you'll see," I assured her.

"You'd better be," she said with all seriousness and walked off.

I wanted to leave the practice immediately and burst out into tears. But weakness was not allowed here. I'd have to save my tears for later. Grind time began now.

Dear Diary,   *Wednesday June 11ᵗʰ*

I had to get over the anxiety of having to present a lesson to my science class and quickly! I still had a few days to deliver on that assignment yet the clock was ticking on my accomplishing these body goals.

I decided today would be the day I'd visit the school fitness center. Not only did I need to snag myself a man, I also needed to work out. These pounds aren't gonna drop themselves.

Dressed in a Victoria's Secret Pink sweatshirt and sweatpants, I felt good walking in the room all bright and confident.

One thing I had learned from my friends is, confidence is key. No matter how you actually feel about yourself, it's best you don't let anyone know you have a negative body image. They will read it all over your face and treat you as such.

I wanted Troy to see my beautiful smile, my adoring personality, and my impeccable taste in fashion. I wanted him to experience my mind and take my body as a work in progress.

I had watched him throughout this year, in and out of the weight room every day afterschool. His grind was hard. Everyone was chatting about how he was rejected from the football team for the past 2 years because of his size. Word through the halls was that he would have a chance to play varsity during his Junior year if he was able to pass the physical test.

I hadn't known what he looked like 2 years ago but I've witnessed his progression over the past year and liked what I saw. Troy was on his way to the varsity team and his determination to do so was impressive to me. After my warning from the cheerleading co-captain, I could relate to his determination.

"You need help with something?" Troy asked with concern.

Apparently, I had walked into the weight room and was standing in place watching him bench press for quite some time.

As embarrassed as I was, I stuttered a response. "Just trying to see how that machine is used. Thanks for the demo…" I then turned around to leave.

"You don't wanna try it? I'm practically finished," he replied.

"Uh, I would probably hurt myself. I'm no where near as strong as you."

"I can help you find your strength limit. C'mon over here. I can tell you undoubtedly wanted to try it," he insisted.

I was hesitant to move closer to him. But he had already caught me red-handed staring him down. The only way to save face was to try using the darn machine. Especially if it would give me an opportunity to speak to him a little more.

I walked over and sat down as he instructed me to.

"What are your fitness goals?" he asked me.

I laughed. "You wouldn't wanna know," I replied.

"Sure I do. Everyone in here has them."

I didn't think he'd be interested in hearing about my insecurities and all. I didn't want to come off as desperate for a change in my physical image as I actually was. So I asked, "what are yours?"

"Aw, you're slick! Well, I've never told anyone this but since we're *both* sharing here, I'll tell you…" He paused and sat down for a moment. Clearly, he was having as hard a time sharing his goals as I was. "Last year when I tried out for the junior varsity football team, I was told I had skills but couldn't play because of my weight."

"Really? That sucks," I interjected. Although I'd heard about this before, it was shocking hearing him admit the blatant truth to me, a perfect stranger.

"Yea, really. Playing football has been a dream of mine since I was a little boy but every time I have an opportunity to play, somebody shuts me down. I couldn't even pass the physical assessment... two years in a row. Not because I'm not strong enough either- but because I was too big to participate in some of the challenges."

"Wow," I sat there stunned. "Well, I think I know what that feels like."

"No way," he replied. "You'd have to take my body for a day to truly understand."

We both laughed. "If I were a man, I'd take your body and turn that flab to a little more flex!" I made a muscle to show him my bicep.

"Oh, wow. You're not playin'!" he touched my arm, impressed.

"Well, I *am* a cheerleader," I blushed. "Those cartwheels don't support themselves."

"I didn't know that."

"You're an athlete and never checked out who's on the squad?" I was stunned. It was rare that anyone at this school hadn't taken notice of the cheerleaders. With all the drama that took place this year and not to mention- us winning the championships- we were kind of a big deal.

"Well, I don't play on any teams so I haven't seen any performances... yet," he smiled.

"Well I hope to see you front in center on the players' bench next game," I smiled.

"That's hopeful thinking. I appreciate that," he smiled. "I think you're done with that machine though."

He helped me out of the weight machine I was pretending to work out at.

"I'm a little embarrassed to say, but I've worked up an appetite," I got up, breathing deeply.

"You already know I'm wit ya!" he laughed. "I'm Troy by the way. Wanna grab somethin' to eat?"

"Morgan, and I'd love to," I accepted. "As long as it's a low calorie meal."

"Man, you're gonna be great for my diet!"

So off we went to *Subway* for sandwiches.

Dear Diary,   *Friday June 13ᵗʰ*

I was in absolute bliss since spending the past few days with Troy. Everyday after school, we met up at the fitness center and had ourselves a workout to remember.

It was cool hanging with someone who understood the pressure I was under to lose weight. He never even asked me again why I was so anxious to shed these pounds. It's like he just gets it.

I was excused from cheerleading today though. One of the captains told me, I needed to get on a treadmill as soon as possible because learning the new routines wouldn't matter if I don't lose at least 15 pounds. *That hurt.*

But when I got to the fitness center and saw Troy, all was well.

I didn't walk up to him immediately. He had his headphones on, focused as ever on one of the cardio machines. So I went on my merry way to do what I had been sent to do.

I found me a treadmill and hardly knew how to turn it on.

Do I just get on and press start? Can I set this thing to make me lose 15 pounds like right now? Do I walk? Do I run?

It was times like this I needed Troy's guidance. But I didn't want to interrupt him today. I truly didn't want to explain why I was even here instead in cheerleading practice. It was quite embarrassing having been sent here under the present conditions.

I looked over to my left to see if there was anyone in the room who could lend me some assistance. But all I saw was a skinny mini chick who did not seem like she belonged here. Then, I glanced over to my right and saw another girl perfectly in shape. It boggled my mind to see these petite little things in the gym, as if they needed to be here making the thick girls feel even more pressure to shed their weight. I was too embarrassed to ask either of them for help.

So I stepped on the machine, determined to figure this thing out on my own.

I started a slow paced walk. In just a moment, the speed began picking up.

Before I knew it, the dang thing had me jogging. *Faster and faster I went!*

I could not control the machine at all! It had me running now. I tried my hardest to maintain my breathing. I started to sweat. I had difficulty catching my breathe.

I wanted to scream out Troy's name but I couldn't open my mouth wide enough to do so. Next thing I knew, I was flying off the machine and across the room. I felt a bump to my head then closed my eyes.

So much for trying to go unnoticed, I thought. By now, everyone had their eyes on me. I was sure Troy and all the skinny girls had seen my big self tumble to the ground. It was awfully humiliating.

I kept my eyes closed to keep myself from bursting out in tears. I listened to the voices to retain my consciousness.

"Do you know her?" a girl whispered.

"No, never seen her here."

"Is that blood on her head? Eww…"

"Well, go call someone. Obviously, we can't lift her up."

"Call the nurse," said a most familiar voice. Troy's. "Tell her Morgan Sawyer had a treadmill accident. They'll have to call her house. I'll have her in the office in just a few."

I felt Troy's strong arms lift me up and carry me swiftly out of the overly air conditioned room. The temperature rise from the school hallway took a toll on me immediately. And then, I lost all consciousness.

Dear Diary, *Saturday June 14ᵗʰ*

Waking up in my bedroom, I smiled with glee thinking of my last memory. Troy rescued me. That is, until I felt a throbbing headache.

I put my hand to my head and realized I had been bandaged up with gauze and tape. *Darn,* I thought, *how bad did I fall?*

My mother was the first person to enter my room after my awakening.

"How are you feeling, honey?" she asked softly.

"Like a failure, mom."

"What? Why would you say that, hon'?"

"I will most likely be kicked off the squad now. The only reason I had this awful accident is because the Captain sent me to the exercise room during practice. She told me I needed to lose weight and-"

"What?! You are perfectly fine the way you are, Morgan. Don't let anyone tell you different."

"That's very sweet of you mom," I lowered my head with shame. "But the standards for a teenage girl are different than they are for you. And I am not even close to meeting them."

"Stop it, honey. *Nobody* is perfect. Not even *one* of those cheerleaders. So don't allow any of them to make you feel like you have to be like them. You are beautiful and talented and if that's not enough for those girls, you can easily walk away."

"I wish it were that easy," I mumbled, knowing my mother would never understand. She has no idea what the competition is like for a high school girl.

"No one promised you life would be easy, Morg. There will always be challenges. Luckily, you have all the power you need to beat them," she encouraged.

That was hard to believe. "Apparently not enough power to work a treadmill, though."

My mother chuckled. "There are other ways to lose weight, you know."

"Oh yea? Tell me the fastest!" I sat up excitedly.

"The *fastest* way is not an option for a teenage girl. But I will share the most *effective* ways. Next time I go grocery shopping, I'll show you. Heck, I may even have to get you into a pool one of these summer days."

I rolled my eyes and sunk back into my pillow.

My mother still hasn't bought into the idea of me having a weight loss operation. Clearly, it was not up for discussion either. She got up to dismiss herself from my room.

If she thinks I have the time or the will to change my diet, she's sadly mistaken. That pool party of the year is only days away. And those cheerleaders are probably making decisions to drop me right now as we speak.

I got on the internet as soon as my mother left. I looked up "ways to appear slimmer" immediately. Some really cool swimwear lines came up while I searched. *Rosegal* and *OMG swimwear*. These were my kind of styles. They seemed to snatch in some waistlines and compliment some curves. Oh and the cover ups were *everything*!

If my mother would just hand over her credit card, I might be a step closer to the confidence she's expecting to see in me.

I could negotiate getting another swimsuit if my upcoming score report was on point. So I picked out a cute two-piece that complimented my large hips and left it in my online shopping cart. Then, I got to working on my science class presentation for Monday.

VOLUME 7: POOL PARTY

Dear Diary,   Wednesday June 20th

It was my first day back to school after recovering from my head injury. I had anxiety all day.

If I wasn't so determined to get that extra credit from my science teacher, I would've taken off for a *few* more sick days.

But there I was, with a huge bruise on my head and a presentation to put on. I hope no one knew what happened to me on Friday during my afterschool exercise. It would literally add insult to injury if people were talking about it.

My teacher called me up to present my lesson on one of the units he covered. I choose to report on the Digestive system. It was pretty clear cut. Plus I actually remembered the name of each organ our food passes through from the mouth to the rectum. LOL. I could easily ace this.

It wasn't until the very end when I had to conduct the Q&A. That was when things got tough.

"Yes," I agreed my classmate. "You have a question."

"What about people who eat too much? What happens to lhe extra food?"

A few students giggled. I couldn't help but blush with embarrassment.

Were they throwing shade at me? Was that a dig at my weight? Were they trying to call me fat?

"The excess food?" I repeated, stalling for time.

"Yea, where does it go?"

I was speechless for a moment. Unsure whether this was a personal attack or a legitimate inquiry, I conjured up a response.

I thought back to my conversation with my mom. She said life wouldn't be easy. She told me I had the power to beat any challenge. And so, that's what I attempted to do.

"Excess food that is useful to the body will break down and enter the blood stream or our bones. Some may be stored as muscle or fat." I cringed having to say that awful word. "And any food that we don't need will be exited through the rectum. That all happens during the digestive process."

Some of my classmates laughed at the word *rectum* but thankfully no laughed when I said *fat.* I was so glad it was over.

As I collected my visual diagram and note cards, my teacher stopped me from returning to my seat.

"One more hand," he said.

"Yes," I addressed my colleague.

"What happened to your head?" he asked.

The class broke out in silent chatter. I timidly opened my mouth to tell the class I fell. But my teacher put his hand up to interrupt.

"That right there, has nothing to do with today's digestive presentation. Ms. Sawyer, you may proceed to your seat. Job well done."

The class applauded as I returned to my seat. *Whew!* Mr. Granger really saved me there! What a finale.

I was excited to leave this class today, knowing I had done well. Good grade, here you come!

Dear Diary,   Friday June 20th

Tuesday had come. It was the last day of cheerleading practice so the girls were having a pizza party.

I didn't bother joining in on that. I would probably be body shamed for eating extra carbs in front of the whole team. Instead, I went to the exercise room to check for Troy. It would be the first time I see him since the accident last week. And I never got to thank him for coming to my aide.

There he was stretching on a floor mat when I walked in. The guy was truly focused.

I walked over to him, a bit nervous.

"Hey Troy."

He finished up his current set of toe touches before turning around to address me.

"Morgan! You're alive," he smiled and got up from his sitting position. He reached his arms open to give me the warmest bear hug.

His arms were smooth and calming. All anxieties I felt were quickly disappearing. I even felt a muscle or two flex up while I was in his hold. I felt all tingly inside.

"Yes, I survived. Thanks to you," I replied with a smile.

"That was pretty scary, girl. What were you thinking getting a treadmill not knowing how?"

"It looked easy enough to me."

"Not at all. You see all those buttons and numbers? They all mean something. They have to be set up before you even start." He walked me over to the machine to explain it more clearly. "Based on your body type and goals, you have to set a level. And you should probably start at the lowest one to see what you can handle."

He started clicking away at the buttons.

"Oh, wow." I tried to focus in on what he was doing. "Didn't know there was such an art to this."

"Yes, there is. It's more of a science though," he laughed.

"Okay, okay. Mr. Know-it-All," I teased.

"I'll take that title, any day. I spend enough time up in here."

He continued to play around with the treadmill until it was time for me to jump on.

"You ready to give it another try?"

"Not sure," I said apprehensively. "I'm still recovering from the last try."

"This time, I got you though." He stood behind the treadmill where he could catch me if I were to fall again. "And if at any point I'm not, you just jump up on the sides..." He demonstrated by opening his legs and jumping onto the side borders, "like this."

I appreciated him spending all this time making sure I got it right. "Okay, it's definitely worth another try then."

I got back on that scary machine and started to move at a much more moderate pace than I remembered.

"This is the warm up pace," he explained. "It will speed up a bit then will go slower for the cool down when you're just about done."

"You really know your stuff, huh?"

"Yea, I mean, I been at this weight loss thing for a while. Though I haven't made as much progress as I would've liked, I could probably train others at this point."

"What kinda progress are you looking to make?" I inquired.

"Just enough to get on the football team," he replied.

"Well, I'm proud of you just for trying."

"I can say the same to you," he smiled.

As I continued to pick up speed, I smiled back. It was truly a motivation to have this amazing new friend of mine encourage me to keep moving. None of my other friends even knew the struggle I was facing. They certainly couldn't get me through it.

After the cool down Troy referred to earlier, he led me over to a bicycle. He said this one was called an elliptical and would work my lower body.

Again, he took a chunk of time out of his own workout regimen to explain how it works.

"I think I got the hang of it, Troy. Thanks. Now don't let me hold you up any further..." I tried to free him from my training session so he could focus on his.

"Alright, Morgan. But you know I'll have my eye on you," he side eyed me as he walked away.

"No doubt," I smiled. I turned around to check out his physique as he walked away. This was truly an amazing guy. Even with his overly wide shoulders and a slight gut hanging over his shorts, I felt an attraction toward him in that moment. No one had ever showed such care and concern toward me. No one had related to me so quickly and non-judgmentally. It felt great.

I turned back around to ride this elliptical machine like it was nobody's business!

After both working up a sweat, Troy and I met back at the stretch mats.

"Oh my gee!" I exclaimed. "How much more of this is it gonna take to lose 15 pounds!"

"Fifteen pounds?" he replied. "How much time do you have?"

"I have about 1 week until the pool party of the year. And about 2 months before the cheer coaches decide whether or not to keep me on the squad..." There, I had finally admitted the motivation behind me being here.

He seemed stunned. "Oh, that's what this is all about?"

I nodded shyly.

"I get the whole squad thing. That's your passion. But the pool party? You can't change your body for those folks! And certainly not in a week."

I knew he was right. All my efforts thus far would be in vain. I guess I'd have to do something a bit more drastic than exercising.

"I mean, I gotta look right for the party though. Are you even going?"

"Hell yea, I'm going! Kendrick is one of my brother's best friends. So we definitely in there!"

"Really? And you have a brother?"

"Yes ma'am. A twin brother at that. But we damn sure don't look alike."

"What do you mean?" I asked.

"Well, he has more athletic body type. And he actually made the team he tried out for..."

"Oh yea?" my curiosity awakened. "What team is that?"

"Basketball of course. He's a natural."

"I know how that is. My sister is a natural athlete too. She plays tennis all over town. She kicks butt, actually." I raved about my sister and her exceptional abilities. I knew how Troy must have felt to live in the shadow of his twin brother's remarkable talents. It was a daily struggle I still had to endure.

"That's what's up," Troy said. He wasn't the least bit discouraged though. "If our siblings can do it, why can't we?!"

"Because they got that athlete's gene and we don't," I replied.

"Speak for yourself," he said. "You can only do what your mind tells you. And I know I'm gonna rock out on the team next year. I just gotta stay working."

I admired his confidence. I envied his determination. I had lost all of mine.

"If you say so." I got up, tired of the slow process we were undertaking to achieve our body goals. "Ain't there other ways to work it, though?"

"Healthier eating is all we got," he got up and replied.

"That works. And I *am* hungry. Let's get to it."

And off to Subway we went for sandwiches.

Dear Diary,   *Saturday June 21ᵗʰ*

The pool party is one week away!

When I showed my parents my science presentation grade, they allowed me to order the swimsuits I left in my shopping carts. Thankfully, I would have a few attractive swimwear options for this infamous event. Whichever of them would tuck and trim my curves down to create the best illusion of slimming sexiness, would be the one I choose.

While I awaited the rush delivery of these new items, I knew there were still matters I needed to take into my own hands.

Everyone had been telling me I needed to curb my eating. They said I needed to eat healthier. I was trying my darn-dest though, and nothing worked.

As I weighed myself in Daphne's and my shared bathroom today, I was face to face with the awful truth. I hadn't lost one pound.

All that exercising and lean meat eating I'd done these past few days was breaking me down. It had me feeling weak, left me hungry, and still hadn't made an inch or a pound of difference.

What more would I have to do?

I called out to my mom who seemed to always have the answers. She was down in the kitchen doing her weekend housework.

She was preparing a deliciously scented brunch for us all. I could smell the seasoned eggs, cinnamon spices, and buttery toasted bagels the minute my foot touched the stairs.

My mother always knew how to throw down!

Too bad this wasn't the week I could indulge in it all. Despite my fond desire to gobble every dish up, I needed to practice a little discipline.

When the entire family was seated at the breakfast table, my mother said her table prayers to bless the food. Even Daphne was home to join us for this meal. My dad came down late but smiled at the marvelous tastings before him. We were all in for a treat.

I searched the table for some greens. There was a small salad placed in the center. There always is. But after taking a few bites and still possessing a massive craving for more, I couldn't help but dig into the carbs. Especially while everyone was raving about the splendor of its taste.

"Darling! You really put your foot in it this time!" my dad exclaimed.

"Doesn't she always?" Daphne replied. "This is *everything* a girl needs before a match."

I couldn't help but indulge. I didn't hold back from the cinnamon rolls and loaded eggs. Nor did I resist the bacon strips and buttered breads. My mother cooked Saturday breakfast like it was an all out feast for the multitudes. And oftentimes, I ate that way.

After it was all said and done, Daphne dashed away to prepare for her tennis match today. She was lucky to have the opportunity to burn off her entire caloric intake by playing hours worth of tennis.

Unfortunately, I was doomed to go back to bed and let them fester in my gut. Or maybe my arms. Or even my thighs. I felt like a huge disgrace.

Laying down a few minutes made me feel sick. *How could I have eaten so much? And all that a week before I put on a bathing suit? What was I thinking?*

There was no doubt in mind that I'd need to forgo everything I had just consumed.

When I heard Daphne finishing up her shower, I hurried to the door.

"Hurry up!" I yelled through the door. "I'm not feeling well! I need to get in there!"

"Hold up a minute!" she yelled back.

Soon after, she came scurrying out all wrapped up in her towel and clutching her clothes.

I rushed inside and heard her utter, "Morgan, you really need to stop overeating."

I couldn't believe she had just said that to me. As if I could control eating the sustenance that were laid out on our table each day. *Would that even be polite to refuse my mother's delicious concoctions?* I think not.

I thought it would be much less rude to lock myself in the bathroom and purge it out after. So that's exactly what I did. Salad and all.

Dear Diary,   *Sunday June 22nd*

My mother woke me up bright and early today to come with her to church again.

"I promised you a grocery trip, didn't I? Well, today's the day!" she shook me out of bed excitedly.

"Do we have to get up this early though?" I resisted.

"I'm going straight after the service so get up now. Let's go!" She pulled the covers all the way off of me.

Ugh! I thought.

My mother always kept a promise. She was a committed woman- to her church, her family, and her word.

So I knew that if I could get my butt out of bed, the entire day hanging with my mother would be worthwhile.

I showered and got dressed as quickly as I could. I wore a knee length pleated skirt with a plain white blouse and a bow tied ribbon around my neck. My mother was impressed by my fashionable church attire.

"Well, well, well!" she exclaimed. "My big girl certainly cleans up nice. Who are you trying to impress today?"

"The Lord," was all could say. We laughed. "He hasn't seen me in a while..."

"You got that right. The entire congregation at that!"

In the kitchen, there was a huge bowl of chopped up fruits. Pineapples, grapes, blackberries, strawberries, and more were delightfully placed on the counter.

"Is that supposed to be breakfast?" I pinched up my face, surprised to see there were no bagels or breads or biscuits.

"Yes, honey. There's yogurt in the fridge if you want to mix it with the fruit. I want to start cutting down on calories but definitely don't want to slack on flavor."

"I could dig it!" I took a large bowl and poured my yogurt inside. Then poured as many fruits as could fit in my bowl. I gobbled it up in minutes. *Delicious* and *filling*, I thought.

"I'm heading outside, big girl. Let's get going," mom said.

I have always known my mother to call me various pet names. And I'm pretty certain they are all terms of endearment. But something about being called, "big girl" didn't sit well with me anymore.

I know I'm the bigger sister and I know I'm the bigger of the girls but could there be more truth to it than that?

As I sat down in the passenger's seat of the car, I had to inquire.

"Mom, why do you call me 'big girl'?" I asked.

"Morgan, has that gotten you down this morning?" she looked over at me now lowering my head. I was ashamed of what I had accused my mother of. "I called you baby girl for years and years until one day, you stopped me and said, 'I'm not a baby anymore!' Since then, I've called you my big girl. Why else would I call you that?"

"I dunno. I thought it had something to do with my size..." I replied. My lowered head was looking out the window.

"Oh no, honey pie. Your size is fine. And I would not use words to convey anything otherwise."

"I feel you, Mom. It's all love," I finally came to understand.

"You know it," she looked me in the eye as we parked.

Attending church once in a blue moon was delightful.

You'll see a person or two that you recognize. You'll sit and enjoy the familiar music. You'll listen intently to every word.

Afterwards, we hopped out at a local supermarket.

My mother gave me a light lecture about the food groups and how to ration them out. She suggested I try to eat a dairy, a grain, a protein, a fruit, and a vegetable everyday. So we collected items from each category. Milk, cheese and yogurt for dairy. Wheat bread and whole grain rice. Lean meats and fish for protein. Assorted fruits and greens for days. My mother collected a few spices and threw them in the cart.

"These are what I call, secret ingredients," she giggled.

"Morgan and mommy classified!" I high fived her.

It was a great day out as expected. And when we got home, she showed me how to throw it all down in the kitchen. We delivered a hearty, healthy feast for the family tonight!

Dear Diary,   *Thursday June 26th*

The last day of school, *at last*!

Everyone was buzzing around about Kendrick's pool party this weekend. People were making summer plans. I was trying to say goodbye to my crew. We all shared photos of our bathing suits for Saturday.

None of the girls knew about my newfound friendship with Troy. I mean, it wasn't that serious anyway.

So when the girls and I were chatting in the hallway and he approached me, it was a bit awkward.

"And you are?" Tammy stepped up to him to guard me.

With all his confidence, he said, "Troyy and you?"

"Hey Troy," I interjected. Tammy backed up a bit to give us space. He came in for a hug. *Those bear hugs were everything!*

"Who's your friend, Morgan?" Patricia asked.

"This is Troy. I met him in the weight room."

"When did you start going to the gym?" Tiffany asks.

"When the cheerleading captains started making me. And no more questions please!" I had enough of their prying.

"Troy, this is Patricia, Tammy, and Tiffany. My crew."

"Nice to meet you all. Anyone going in that pool Saturday?" he asked.
The girls all looked at each other and said in unison, "Are we?!"

"Yea," said Tammy. "We are showing up *and* showing out!" She and Patricia high five.

Speak for yourselves, I thought. Their bodies were all the way right. I couldn't speak so boldly.

"I like your vibe," Troy addressed the group. "Morgan, just a sec'." He motioned me over to the side.

"What's up Troy?"

"Not much. Just wanted to make sure you're setting up your summer goals. I don't want you to break you exercise routine yet."

"Exercise in the summer?" that was something I'd never done.

"Yea, I'm gonna be training all summer long. And you could do it too," he continued.

"I don't know about that, Troy. My family is supposed to be going away half the summer." As I looked back at my friends, I saw them staring.

"Okay, well. I just want you to do whatever you can to stay on your cheer team. I know what it's like to have that determination. Don't give up now."

"You're right. I won't."

"I'll be training and coaching at Push fitness facility from noon to four Monday through Thursday all summer long. Join me sometime. I'll even let you lead a routine one day."

"Really?" that last part really excited me. "Okay, let's do it."

We fist pounded to seal the deal.

"See you Saturday. You're gonna look great," he said with a wink. I was all smiles as we parted ways.

Dear Diary,   *Saturday June 28ᵗʰ*

The day had come. My swimsuits had arrived!

I was just trying them on when Daphne came on in.

"What is this lingerie that you wearing today..?" she came closer eying my two-piece swimwear.

"It's a bathing suit if you must know. And obviously this one's to small for me. Next!" I struggled to get it off.

"Are you going swimming?" she asked.

"Oh, yes. Pool party at a friend's house. Are you trying to come?" I hoped she wasn't.

"Nah, I wanted to know if you wanted to come practice with me today. We're having informal drills."

"Aww, nice. An invitation," I appreciated. "Unfortunately, this is not a party I can miss. Rain check?"

"Sure thing!" she was unbothered.

Before she left, I needed her to approve my final pick of these swimsuits.

"Nah, not that one sis'. There's a little too much junk peeping through that trunk."

Well, I couldn't knock her for being honest. I frowned at myself in the body length mirror across the room, wanting so badly to alter my view.

"I guess the third one will be a charm!" I tried on the final swimsuit, hoping this one didn't expose too much but still emphasized my curves. Not the rolls in my stomach nor my love handles either.

"Yup, that's the one!" Daphne confirmed.

It was a low cut v-neck pink piece. My back was exposed but just enough to hide those side rolls, excess belly fat and junk in my trunk. Daphne tightened the back for me until I could no longer breathe with ease.

"That's good," I stammered out trying to take a deep breath.

"You sure?" she asked.

"Do I look sure?" I needed her final opinion.

"Yes, Morg'. You look amazing!"

That was all I needed. "Thanks D. Good luck today, as if you ever need it."

She smiled with satisfaction and left my room. I continued to ready myself with body oils and bronzer. I sprayed on my sunscreen and added a little eye shadow to my face. Then I threw on a pair of jeggings. I was dressed to impress.

Not long after, I heard my ride honking. Tammy had arranged a car service to pick us all up.

Inside the car, I was filled with jealousy to see the other girls with their cleavage perfectly placed and stomachs tight and glowing. I had never seen Patricia this way, with short shorts and a bikini top tied in the center of her chest. Tammy was in a silver studded one piece with cutouts at her navel, bosom and sides. She wore a netted cover up that was long like a dress and left nothing to the imagination. My girls looked good.

"Where's Tiffany?" I asked noticing her absence.

"Not coming again. She thought her swimsuit would fit over that belly but failed to realize it would grow significantly over the past few weeks," Tammy replied.

"We will have to party hard in honor of her," I said. "What are we drinking girls? Sprite? Pepsi?"

"Glad you asked," Tammy said deviously. "I snagged some bottles from my dad's cellar. And I certainly don't want to try it alone." She handed each of us a glass from the minibar of our ride.

Patricia put her hand up. "I'll pass." She had something against alcohol these days. Who knew what she'd encountered this past year to keep her from having a little innocent fun with her friends.

"Pass it over here!" I raised my glass waiting for her to pour me some.

Once the red liquid reached my lips, it tasted bitter with a hint of dryness. Nothing really appetizing about it.

"You like?" Tammy asked.

"Not really," I said trying to consume the small amount she had poured.

"That means you need more," she insisted. "It's not about the flavor anyhow. It's more about the way it makes you feel."

"How is she supposed to feel?" Patricia asked.

"She's supposed to feel free. It'll make her more comfortable. Like really let go of your insecurities. Be your best self..."

If that's what this is for, I could certainly use some more. I didn't want to encounter anymore jealous staring nor did I want to feel out of place.

I took another swig of this drink and totally felt more at ease.

Tammy pulled out her newest cellphone and motioned us together for a few selfies. I was looking and feeling like my best self indeed.

When we arrived at Kendrick's house, we were impressed by the perfectly cut hedges and richly green landscaping. His 3 story home was made of light brown bricks and designed with 2 brick pillars standing tall at his front door.

Just as we were about to ring the bell, we were instructed by a party staffer to walk around the house and straight to the backyard.

The music from his hired DJ was already blaring the latest pop tunes. There were beach chairs lined up surrounding every inch of the pool. Food platters were still covered and set up on the lawn under white linen tents.

We had arrived right on time! We had first pick of the beach chairs and selected the ones closest to the pool deck.

"Pass me that bottle," I enjoyed the feeling Tammy's drink made me feel and wanted more as I lay under the blazing sun.

"Better slow down," Patricia warned me. "That stuff can take away your ability to think straight or even move."

"I'll slow down after this, I promise."

Not too long after we'd arrived and were all comfortably seated, some upper classmen cheerleaders arrived and sat fairly close to us. They had brought their own bottles to drink as well.

It wasn't long before their brown bottles landed into my hands. I could not refuse a taste.

The girls were up and about, dancing to the popping beat of the music. With their slender hips and shiny skin, each and every swimsuit fit these girls like a glove. I longed to exude that level of beauty. And with every sip I took, the more I was able to let those envious thoughts go.

Tammy interrupted my thought to suggest we play a game. "Who would you rather?"

"Who would we rather.. what?" Patricia asked, always a little clueless.

"Be with of course," I replied. "Duh!"

"Yea, like French kiss, touch on, sleep with," Tammy clarified.

"Y'all know I have eyes for only one man," Patricia cooed.

"My Diesel boo. And I hope he gets out of the hospital soon."

"Happy thoughts, please!" Tammy exclaimed, slightly slurring her words.

"Well, I have never done any of the above," I stated honestly.

"Today is gonna be your lucky day, girl." Tammy pointed over to the pool house positioned on the far side of the lawn. "Take your pick of the guys here today and go do a little experimenting of your own."

"Take my pick?" I have never had choices of dudes.

"Yes, even good girls deserve to have a little fun. Ask

Patricia, she knows..."

"Don't ask *me* nothing!" Patricia replied. "The only experimenting I'd ever want to do again is to conjure up true love."

"Love? What's love got to do with this?!" Tammy said. We laughed.

We both knew the guys in our school well enough to know love was not being offered. We had to take what we could get. And I was pretty sure, Troy would be it for me.

The ball players slowly trickled in and were surrounding the head cheerleaders. I wondered how long it would take for one of them to notice me, if at all.

I was afraid to even stand up and dance. I had found a perfectly complementing way to lay my thick thighs on this beach chair and didn't want to mess up my flow.

But Troy came in and gave me no choice.

"Morgan and company! Meet my brother, Trey." He came over with his twin brother who extended his arms for hugs. Trey was certainly his twin, with identical eyes and complexion. However, his arms were chiseled and his abs were ripped, just as Troy had said. His brother had an athlete's body indeed.

Trey had an equally infectious personality as his brother. "What are you daredevils drinking over here? Doesn't smell legal to me!" He was on to us.

"Don't ask questions and we just may pour you some," Tammy teased.

"Say no more," Trey went to retrieve himself a plastic red cup.

Troy turned his attention to me. "You look amazing in that

suit, just I had imagined you to be."

I wish I could say the same to him. But his bulging belly was more obvious with his swim trunks tightly pulled around his waste and a netted tank loosely worn over it, exposing his entire upper body. *He should have covered all that* up, I thought. I was a bit turned off actually.

"Thanks Troy," I barely looked his way. "I know how to display my body tastefully. You should consider it sometime."

"What is that supposed to mean?" he was puzzled by my cold response.

"You're showing too much and it isn't cute," I said, stunned at my own blatant honesty.

"Well damn. Never knew you felt that way..."

I was unbothered by his crushed feelings. "Well, now you know. Wanna go make out in the pool house?" I was certainly behaving more boldly than ever before.

"Not sure," he side eyed me. "Let me grab a hot dog first. I'll be right back."

Someone must have overheard our conversation. A whole crowd was attentive to the comments that came after.

"What the hell is wrong with this dude?!" one of the football players shouted. "He's checking for a hot *dog* when he could have a hot *chick!*"

"The guy's got his priorities off."

"No wonder his fat ass can't get on the team."

I knew why he'd chosen to grab a bite to eat. He knew I was acting strange. I could have defended him, but I didn't have the guts. Especially when the cheerleaders jumped into this roasting.

"Can any one of you fine *straight* men break Morgan off today? The girl needs some positive male motivation for the summer..."

I didn't know what that meant.

"Break me off?" I looked at my friends. Tammy smiled with encouragement while Patricia shook her head with shame.

"Take your pick," Tammy repeated.

Trey interjected, "You guys are not about to call my brother no more names. Lay off him or you all gon' have to deal with me."

The basketball team members got silent. The football players laughed.

One uttered, "we ain't never scared!"

"Keep it up and I'll change your mind," Trey continued.

The basketball team members stood up to defend Trey. The football players backed down. So Trey walked away to check on his brother.

"Tough crowd," one of the girls laughed. "Can't we all just get along?"

I was ashamed and embarrassed by what had just transpired. Because of me, Troy was at the butt end of an evil joke and his brother Trey almost got into a fight. I was frozen in place trying to decide my next move.

"Okay, that show's over," Tammy pointed out. "Is anyone actually getting in the pool?"

"Me!" Patricia replied. "I thought you'd never ask. Didn't think you folks actually get down like that into the water."

"Oh, I'm down," Tammy said. "Already made me a hair appointment for tomorrow. You coming Morgan?"

"Nah, I don't know how to swim. This is the closest I've come to being in a pool since I was a child. You guys go ahead though. I'll take pics."

"Alrighty then! You're gonna miss out on this beautiful water touched by that hot sun? Not to mention an awesome workout? Suit yourself!"

"I'll watch and maybe learn something from you girls."

My friends looked amazing jumping into the pool water with their skimpy swimwear on. It was no wonder how our crew- being just freshmen- got so much attention from our peers. I would never get this kind of love on my own.

And though I could very well swim, I was in no shape to receive the attention they were encountering.

I continued sipping on the drinks going around. I took tons of photos of the girls from Tammy's phone. I took photos of the DJ in his booth, the crowds coming in, the awesomely cut grass, and a few pictures of myself.

As I snapped one last picture, someone jumped in.

"Photobomb!" he exclaimed.

"Who's that?" I turned around ready to turn up.

"Hey chill, it's me Trey. Delivering a friendly reminder that my brother deserves an apology."

"You're absolutely right. And you deserve a thank you," I gave him my fist for a pound.

"We good. But my brothers in that pool house waiting for his apology."

I looked toward the pool house and saw the light flick on and off. Then looked at my friends in the water having their fun without me.

I decided to grab a quick bite and walk into the pool house. I was ready to give Troy what he was waiting for. After all, he was my top pick. He didn't deserve the things I'd said earlier.

When I eventually, walked in, I got right down to business in the dark. I was weak and incoherent so he helped lead my body to his.

Before long, my mind began to wonder if I were truly with Troy. His touch was rough and his speed was fast.

Then, someone abruptly turned the lights on. I looked up and saw Troy watching me in awe.

I had been set up. It was the most embarrassing moment of my life. My first time was with a complete stranger instead of a dude most deserving of me.

"Just wanted you to know what kind of whores these girls are, bro," Trey walked in after patting his twin brother's shoulder and gave his friend a handshake. "Even the big girls."

It was the sickest joke I'd ever witnessed. I ran to the bathroom to rid my body of this liquid waste burning in my stomach. As I hung my head over the toilet, no one came to my aide.

I could only imagine, Troy was distraught once again. There was no apologizing now. We both needed to escape.

VOLUME 8: GETAWAY

Dear Diary,   **Monday June 30th**

Thankfully, my family goes on annual vacations every summer. This year we unanimously voted on an exotic Caribbean island. So in a few short hours, we'd be off on a plane and whisked into paradise for an entire month.

It was therapeutic to leave the bad vibes behind and enter a place of serenity and resort stewards.

As we sat in the airport, I couldn't help but feel a few negative vibes near.

I looked over at my sister who was tapping her feet to the beat blaring from her headphones. Then at my parents who were scowling at each other. They looked equally pissed.

I knew this wasn't the time or place to intervene on anyone's current status so I closed my eyes to rest up for this trip.

The next time we speak, I'll be on Caribbean land!

Dear Diary,   **Tuesday July 1st**

This place is bliss!

The resort is amazing! My sister and I are sharing a room adjacent to my parents suite. The all-inclusive dinner options are delicious. The excursions look adventurous. The skies were bright and blue.

As we sat to enjoy our first vacation dinner as a family, my father brought up a controversial topic.

"While we are all here living our best lives, I need you to remember that your health still matters."

"Oh course it does, honey." My mother continued to dig in to her plate.

"Especially yours darling," he continues. "I want to see you all eating much healthier and working out more regularly."

"Excuse me?" my mother took the words out of my mouth.

"You heard me," Dad said. "This family is going to be eating much differently from now on."

"I don't think so Manuel," Mom said sternly.

Daphne and I looked at each other in shock.

"Listen, I'm not going to continue to watch my wife and kids blow up like cows. So I'm putting my foot down here and now. If you aren't exercising, you better be watching your diet!"

My mother was astonished by my father's words. She couldn't find another word to utter.

"Really, Dad?" I interjected.

"Sorry honey, I want the best for you all and this is it. No more meat for you, no sugary juices, and no bread. While we're on this trip, I want to see you take part in a physical activity every morning and every evening. That is how you'll earn allowances while we're here."

It was actually the strict motivation that I needed. Maybe this is a lifestyle change that may actually work.

"So you're serious?" I asked again.

"As I'll ever be." My dad was not playing around. He was truly unhappy with the weight my mother and I had gained over the years. Daphne was living proof that exercise worked and he was determined to see us through it.

"What are my dietary constraints, Dad?" Daphne asked him jokingly.

"More protein, Daph and less sugars," he replied.

"Oh Mr. Ruler, what are my laws?" my mother asked sarcastically.

"You and I can talk later. Enjoy the rest of your dinner," he attempted to calm her down.

"No thank you," she got up abruptly. "I would like to excuse myself." And just like that, she was gone.

Dear Diary,   *Saturday July 5th*

Daphne and I had no problem following my father's orders. She was eating more meat and I was eating much less. That is, until the Teen Party this weekend.

Down by the beach, every teen at the resort gathered around a huge fire pit for music, games, and tons of food.

There was fish frying, jerk chicken grilling, and pork roasting all night long. I just had to try it all!

There was corn, fried dumplings, seasoned rice, and everything nice. Then for dessert, they offered an assortment of frozen ice flavors, ice cream with a variety of toppings, and banana bread with the option of adding whipped cream on top. I was in an exclusive part of heaven, where a curvy girl shouldn't have been. But I thanked God for allowing me here.

I silently prayed that my dad wouldn't come through checking on us. If he did, I was doomed!

I had already begun pigging out at this party. In just another moment, I would be back at the grill for more. Even with Daphne in my ear, warning me about the food I was eating, I couldn't stop.

I was out of control!

It wasn't until we were approached by a few of the town locals that I curbed my eating for a moment.

They came up to us as we danced to the reggae tunes and swayed with the warm night's breeze.

"You nah wan spicy drink?" one of the guys said in his exotic accent.

"Spicy drink?" my sister asked. "I like a little spice."

"Take a taste," one of them offered.

"Wait," I reminisced back to the pool party and the awful effects those "spicy drinks" had on me. I could not be held responsible for my little sister undergoing similar trauma. "Let me try it first."

"You're always having all the fun!" she complained.

"Believe me, it isn't always 'fun' I'm having. I'm trying to protect you, sis'."

As I brought that little swig to my lips, the smell alone intoxicated me. It was strong but deliciously sweet. "What do you call this?" I asked.

"Rum punch," they replied. "Exclusive mix only fi this land."

I drank it all up. Daphne was super curious to try it and at this point, I couldn't stop here.

"Ohhh, an adult drink," she quickly picked up on. "We'll buy two." Daphne reached out a wad of Caribbean cash and paid the local salespeople.

"You are gonna get us in trouble," I said.

"We're in a whole other country, Morgan. We don't even know what's right and wrong on this island. Have a little fun!" And she continued her dancing while sipping on her rum drink.

I couldn't forget the awful feeling I had in my stomach when I'd consumed as much as I did as the pool party. There was no way I would allow any drink to take so much control over me again.

So I made it my business to keep a close watch on my sister. She was having a blast and nothing I did or said was slowing her down from her ecstasy.

I made myself another ice cream sundae to fill this ultra craving that came about. This time, I added chocolate and caramel syrup, cookie crunches, marshmallows, strawberries, and whipped cream on top.

I decided if I danced out here long enough, I would have fulfilled an additional physical activity for the day and these calories would burn right off.

Wrong! Just minutes into my dance craze, I caught a cramp. I felt bloated and gassy. I needed to take a seat.

Daphne was oblivious to me now, as I expected her to be. I wanted so badly to get her attention but she was whisked away into a crowd of people, shaking her tail feather.

All I could do was find a nearby receptacle, hang my head over it, and rid my body of all the excess food bringing me this pain.

Having flushed my system out, yet again, I regained the strength to find Daphne.

I pulled her from the crowd and uttered, "It's time to go. I don't want mom or dad to come looking for us. Especially not like this."

"Okay, okay," she garbled out. "You're killing my vibe anyway."

We held onto each other as we walked up the beach toward the hotel, our long skirts blowing behind us with the night's air.

Home sweet home, I thought as we neared the light of the resort door.

On our floor, we heard a loud commotion. Daphne and I looked at each other hoping these voices weren't as familiar as they seemed.

But the closer we got, the truth was apparent. Our parents were fighting again.

"What are we gonna do?" I whispered to my sister.

"Get to our room as quickly as we can and mind our mother loving business," she replied. It was always her remedy for conflict.

"Alright, okay," I agreed. Our parents had been going at it way too much recently and neither or us were in a state of mind to assist right now.

We needed to get away from the drama. And so into our room we went to silence it all.

Dear Diary,   *Thursday July 10*[th]

We woke up this morning excited to take part in a family excursion. We rented a yacht for the day to take us on a tour of the ocean. We had our paddle boat, snorkeling suits and fishing poles onboard and ready to go.

I put on the most suitable swimsuit I had. It was a lot more comfortable than the it was the last time I tried it on. Maybe I had lost an inch. ☺

The morning started out beautifully. The sun sat like a crown amongst the clear blue skies. Breakfast was attractively laid out on the top deck.

I wasn't allowed to drink the orange juice nor eat the bagels so I stuck to a fruit salad and granola yogurt bowl. It was absolutely delicious! :-P

There were deck chairs laid out on the front of the boat. We each had a comfortable place to lay down as the captain rode us along the stunning smooth seas. We were off on an adventure. Low music was playing from above.

Our hosts offered us a tour of the entire sea craft. The hostess offered us beverages.

"Ice cold water with lemons and lime," I requested.

"Good choice, baby girl," my father said. I rolled my eyes.

In just a moments time, they were back with it, exactly as I'd ordered.

And in that same time, my parents had begun their quarrelling.

"I still cannot believe you decided to change everyone's eating patterns without speaking to me first," my mother began.

"How many times do we have to discuss this? I am always telling you the overindulgences have got to stop. You never listen. I *had* to take matters into my own hands."

"'Taking matters in your own hands' is not the way we do things. I thought we were a team," Mom replied.

"Well, I certainly don't feel that way these days. You are not understanding how important this is to me," he said sternly. My dad didn't even look my mom's way as she spoke.

"I can't believe you're talking and feeling this way..."

"If these feelings are new to you now, I guess you haven't heard a word I've been saying for the past few years."

"Of course I'd heard you. But what am I to do, stop cooking and catering to this family? Stop doing what I love most?"

My dad was silent for a moment.

I couldn't understand how we could be on this gorgeous island speeding along the clearest blue seas under the calmest skies and not absolutely be appreciating the awesome views.

The image ahead of us was almost too good to be true. It was like a portrait vividly drawn from the detailed view of my eyes. The colors were so illicit and bright as if God painted this perfection Himself. The skyline was a flawless straight line, the sun was beaming brightly. Clouds swam through the sky like ducks in a pond. I lay on my stomach to soak in the vitamin D pouring onto my skin from the sun.

This private boat was a time for the family to bond intimately. But my parents were speaking breakup words in the midst of this most awesome tropical getaway. It didn't make any sense to me. *How were we not all completely enjoying this blissful experience?*

My father lowered his voice and tone as he resumed his conversation with my mother. As I turned over on my back to even out my tan, I strained to hear every word.

"Look honey, I love everything you do for us. But cooking and catering are not the ways to my heart," he said with sincerity. "There are other languages of love that I speak and you're not quite listening."

"Oh really?" my mother questioned.

"Yes," he paused and looked away. "I want to experience

more of a physical connection. More confidence. More touching. And with the way you're moving around here, I don't feel you want to give that to me."

My mother was speechless. I didn't think I should have been hearing this. But only a few short feet away, I couldn't help but ear hustle a bit.

"How can you say that?!" she struggled to keep her voice and tone low so we couldn't hear. "I have given you everything I've got in me to keep you happy. I-"

"Well I'm not happy," he interrupted. And that was the end of that conversation. He turned around on his beach chair with his back to my mom.

Clearly, there was not much more to discuss within earshot of mixed company.

The dramatic silence that followed brought on such awkwardness. Background played as I pretended to be taking photos with the family camera.

"Smile guys!" I motioned to my parents. Neither of them could force a genuine grin. I snapped the picture anyway.

Shortly after, the boat staff called us all to gather at the back of the boat. Daphne who was exercising on the top level came running down.

"We have arrived at the eagle's eye. This is the most shallow location within this sea. You can jump out and swim into one of those caves," the host pointed to a large pack of rocks followed by a rush of down pouring water. "Climb up the waterfall, you can paddleboard around, put on your snorkel and discover the underwater world. Later we will go deeper into the sea to throw a line out for the fish."

It sounded amazing! As I looked down, I could see straight to the bottom of the aqua blue water. I couldn't wait to dive in.

The staff offered us life jackets and gave us safety precautions before allowing us to explore.

Daphne and I took this first chance we could to hold hands tightly and jump right in. We splashed and laughed as the warm water soaked our hair and bodies.

My parents got their snorkels on without saying much of a word and helped each other into the ocean. Down under they went to become one with the clear blue seas.

I hoped for their sake that they would use this opportunity to try and salvage their marriage. There was no better place to delight yourselves in good company than in this peaceful paradise.

Then, like a shocking scare, I caught an uncomfortable cramp in my crotch. "OMG! I can't move!"

Daphne looked my way and saw me frantically attempting to tread the water.

"What happened sis'! Did something bite you?!" she exclaimed.

"I dunno! Just get me out of here!" I squirmed.

"Help!" we screamed while attempting to swim back to the boat.

The staff threw us a lifesaver and Daphne grabbed hold of it to guide me back. The pain never let up.

We rushed to the bedroom to discover where this random pain had come from. The medical aide came inside to check my vitals. I pointed to the area between my legs that caused this awful ache. He gave me some pain relieving cream and an ice pack then tried to diagnose me.

"It seems you have experienced some trauma in the pelvic region."

"What is that supposed to mean?" I asked.

"It appears that you have begun to exercise a muscle surrounding your pelvis recently and the rapid exploration of it today put the muscle in shock."

I knew exactly what this 'recent exercise' was. My virginity was taken and I had not recovered. Then I just jumped out here, shocking my body to another degree.

"So wait, is this gonna happen every time I swim?"

"Not if you are constantly swimming. The more you move these muscles, the less shock they will experience each time. Your body is like a vehicle. If you drive it everyday, it will start with ease. But if you drive once a year or so, each time you try to start it up, it'll stall to get revved up for the ride."

"So the point is...?" Daphne interjected, trying to make sense of the analogy.

"Keep your body in motion," he replied. "Warm it up before exercise, get moving, and cool it down before resting. And by the looks of it, you already understand the concept of movement."

"Yes, she's an athlete," I stated.

"It's quite obvious," he looked at her lean physique and nodded. He could've guessed I was quite the opposite.

"Well, thank you, doc! I will certainly think about what you said." I truly did contemplate on how all the serious athletes planned their workouts. Both Troy and my sister were consistently stretching. It was to my detriment that I would jump into random activity without preparation.

"Ok, spill it!" Daphne said as soon as the medical aide left the room.

"Spill what?" I asked.

"You know this recent and rapid exploration isn't from swimming." My sister side eyed me. "Something else went on down there. And I need to know what."

I hadn't even discussed the awful pool party experience with my friends yet. I wasn't sure I was quite ready to express it to my sister either.

"Morgan!" we heard my parents call my name. Someone had alerted them of my emergency.

"In the room, Mom! And I'm fine!"

"Talk fast," Daphne urged me.

"Not now, Daphne. I don't want anyone hearing this. You know mom and dad will have a fit if they overhear."

"True," she agreed. "But I'll be waiting to hear the details!"

And so I let her wait. After a little rest, she led a pelvis muscle stretch to some awesome music. It was uncomfortable at first but eventually, it felt amazing to get that kink out of my body.

Later on, we fished.

At dinnertime, we stopped off on a private island to enjoy a scrumptiously prepared meal exclusively for us.

After dinner, my family pulled out the paddleboards and got back on the water for a relaxing ride.

Dear Diary,   *Friday July 11ᵗʰ*

Daphne wasted no time getting the details of my recent experience.

She woke me up bright and early today for a sisters day out.

"I ordered us room service for breakfast since I have an early court reserved," she explained. "Time to get up and at it!"

The girl had some serious discipline. Between her timing and her physical pursuits, I could never keep up. So I never tried.

Breakfast arrived and was a tasty surprise. She had ordered me some bagels against our father's wishes.

"I see you snuck in some carbs. What is it you want from me today?" I asked jokingly.

"Only because you will more than burn them off playing a few tennis matches with me today!" She continued, "*and* I'm expecting you to spill some tea. So here it is!" Daphne handed me a green tea bag.

"Oh girl," I knew there was an ulterior motive.

"Spill it!" she insisted.

"Honestly, I don't know where to begin. I don't remember it all. And I'm pretty content not having all the details..."

"C'mon, you gotta give me something. What happened?!"

"I lost my virginity," I hung my head down low. "You happy now?"

"What? Really? To who?"

I was ashamed to admit it. "I don't know. I can't remember."

"That doesn't make any sense."

"I know. That's why I don't wanna talk about it. I've been trying hard not to even think about it..."

"Well, you've got to at least explain why you can't remember!" she urged me.

It took me a minute to collect my thoughts. I had not even taken a moment to reflect on the events that took place during the pool party. It was horrifying and embarrassing.

I hadn't even told my friends about it. All I remembered was drinking too much, hurting the one guy I truly cared about, then mistaking someone else's touch for his. Nothing good came of that day for me so I tried hard to erase it from my memory.

"I had been drinking alcohol... You know that spicy type stuff that adults like. It was disgusting but I didn't want to be the only one not trying it..." I began.

"Oh boy! I remember feeling that way when we were on the beach at the teen party..."

"Yea, I know. That's why I didn't dare allow that stuff to touch my lips," I remembered.

"It didn't seem so bad, though. It just made me feel free."

"Well, sure it did after a few sips. But imagine a few cups. For a moment, it even took away my insecurities..." I hung my head down with shame.

"Shouldn't that be a good thing..?" my sister asked.

"Nope, not when you forget who you are, who you're with, and what you're doing with them. That's exactly what happened to me. And it wasn't worth it. Not for a second."

"Wow, I can't even imagine that," was all she could say.

"Yea," I replied. "And you wouldn't want to."

"Well, when we get back home, sister girl, we will have to get to the bottom of this. You need to know the name of the guy who took you out of the V club. I don't know how you could even rest without that missing piece of your puzzle."

She was right. It was inhumane of me to not to wonder profusely about such an important experience. Something had been taken from me. In essence, something was gone.

A part of me was probably relieved that my virginity was taken altogether. It sucked being the only one in my entire crew who had not had a single encounter with the opposite sex.

Even Patricia the prude had her fair share of pleasure. And although a huge amount of it came with pain, she was lucky to know it at all.

I have been so accustomed to guys shunning away from me. It was finally time to tell my story. Too bad I couldn't remember a single detail.

"For sure," I responded to my sister. "There are a few pieces missing. And I'd love to get the whole picture."

"Consider it done!" she exclaimed. I knew my sister was a determined little girl. It was rare she cared enough to weasel her way into anyone's personal life. She often had much of her own efforts to conquer. So I knew, if she was on the case, it would certainly be cracked.

Reflecting back to that awful experience began to eat away at my esteem. It was a good thing my sister had an action packed day planned out for us on the court. I indulged in her favorite sport to take my mind off of my troubles. Today, I intended to get some weight off my back- literally and figuratively!

Dear Diary,   *Monday July 14th*

Last night, my family enjoyed a lively concert in the

ballroom of the resort. It was awesome!

Some of our favorite reggae artists graced the stage for Carib Fest. The crowd roared in unison as the music blared from the surrounding speakers. I moved to the rhythms of the erupting screams and dance movements. It was an alluring experience to see my favorite celebrity musicians up close and personal and some in their home country. This was an experience to remember!

For some reason, the lights and blaring music began to alter my energy. I was growing tired of standing and jumping. After and hour and a half of the high powered performances, I wanted to get out of there.

After my third yawn, I signaled to Daphne that I needed to step out for a few. She mouthed, "Do you have your key?" and I shook my head, "yes."

In a moments time, I was walking tiredly back to my hotel room. Suddenly, I bumped into an unnervingly familiar face on the way.

Just as I made it past the resort lobby and onto the elevator corridor, I saw a face that I had only caught a glimpse of once before.

"You look familiar." He looked at me and spoke with the exact same candor. I was speechless.

"Patricia, right?" he continued.

I knew who he was. It was the guy from the pool party. *But what in the world was he doing here?!*

The hurtful, malicious occurrence came back to me. *Why would anyone want to use my innocent body and soul that way? And how could I have let them?*

I had questions and I needed answers.

VOLUME 9: REJECTED

Dear Diary,   *Tuesday July 15th*

I had to take a shower since Daphne finally got out. But I'm back...

So dude from the pool party was just checking in with his family. Coincidentally, they came to this *very* island on this *very* day to this particular resort for the Carib Fest concert. I guess it was a huge deal.

His name? "Jay. And I cannot believe I'm getting a chance to say I'm sorry to you," he said.

"Wow," was all I could reply. I was not expecting that at all.

"Do you remember me at all?" he asked.

"Vaguely," I replied.

"Yea, I could figure that. The day was a bit hazy for us all."

That was news to me. And I wanted to know more.

So I answered, "Tell me about it. Were you aware of everything that went down in the pool house?"

We had to grab a seat by the snack bar to continue this conversation.

"Yes," he answered. "But let me explain."

I wondered what words this boy spoke to engage me in further conversation. I was hardly listening to his eager apologies. Because in that very moment, my father crossed my path.

He was walking past the eatery with a woman. His arm was

wrapped around her waist and his lips were on her cheek.

Who was this woman? Who was this man? And what was he thinking?

I could barely see her face well enough to know if she was the same person my father was hugged up with at the Cirque de Soleil show. I did see that he was just as cozy now as he was then.

The vision before my eyes disgusted me. Not only was I tired, now I was sick.

Did my father bring this woman here? Or did he just meet her for a casual encounter?

I knew it wasn't much of my business. But I had to tell someone.

I looked over at this Jay character and thought, *he would never understand.* I hardly knew the root of his own intentions.

"I have to go," I uttered.

"Did you hear *anything* I said?" he asked.

"Yea, sure. And it's okay. I think we both were out of our element. It was just a mistake though. Apology accepted."

"I appreciate that but I don't think you heard me. I don't think it was mistake. I actually enjoyed it," he said.

That took me quite off guard.

"I mean, I guess that's no surprise... You are a boy."

"That's not fair," he replied. "But what did *you* think?"

"Well," I stalled. "The worse part about the whole thing was that I can't remember it. I hardly remember it being with you..."

"Really?" he was shocked to learn this. "Wow, that bites. Who did you think I was?"

I thought about Troy. I pondered whether or not they knew each other, liked each other, or would ever meet. I wondered whether or not this short, fit guy sitting with me had ever passed judgment on him for his size.

"Someone else," was all I could say.

"Wow," he sat there stunned.

"Wait," I thought. "So you knew it was me? Why did you do it?"

"I told you already, I was checking you out and my boys said you wanted me too. Didn't think we'd go all the way in a day but I was glad we did."

This was a lot for me to take in.

This guy Jay was checking for me? That was new. And he actually hadn't tricked me into taking my virginity? He thought it was consented?

"Wow," I said in shock. "Wow, wow."

"That's what I'm saying."

"Okay, this is crazy. But I'm glad I got the whole truth. Thank you for not being a complete jerk like your friends," I said.

"I try," he replied. "So when can we do it again?"

I was taken aback by his plea. "What?"

"You didn't experience the pleasure. And that's not fair to either of us. What do you say?"
I couldn't believe he was serious. It was extremely bold of

him to think I'd consider doing this again. I admired his confidence though. And certainly, what he said made sense.

I had a life changing experience and couldn't recall a single detail except the betrayal of it all.

It wouldn't have been a bad idea to give each other an honestly agreeable encounter. However, I still had some personal business to tend to.

"Look, I'm having a family emergency and really have to go right now. Meet me here, same time tomorrow night and we'll talk."

"Cool," he said. And I was out in a flash.

I hurried as fast as I could to find my sister. I needed to spill out the details of my bittersweet evening.

Still energized at the concert, I found her whining her little body to another high powered performance. Some new Caribbean artist was onstage performing some banger that even I couldn't ignore.

"*Exotic* like a stranga! Likkle hint of danga! Hot like fiyah! Same creator make yuh! Perfect like a sculpture. You nah know mi wan yuh! Show me what you got now! Show me somethin' hot yow!" I couldn't help but rock my head to the beat and twist my hips a bit.

Nonetheless, I pulled her from her spot beside my mother frantically.

"Daphne, I need to tell you something!" I displayed the urgency within my shaking bones.

Finally outside the concert hall, she asked, "What is it? And make it quick!"

"Where did daddy go?"

"He left right after you did. Said he was tired. You're both party poopers," she teased.

"Well, he lied."

"What do you mean?"

"I saw him with a woman."

"A friend, maybe."

I shook my head. "No, like a girlfriend. Hugged up, kissing, arm over the shoulder."

Daphne was not phased. "Morgan, you are always nosing into grown folks' business. Leave daddy alone and let him enjoy his vacation."

"What? You don't see anything wrong with that?"

"It sounds bad, yes. But he and mom haven't been getting along for a while now. We can't expect him to put his whole life on pause to remain unhappy. Mom doesn't care anyhow."

"What makes you think mom wouldn't care to know?" I wondered.

"She knows what the problems are and isn't willing to do anything about it."

I could not believe my ears. Daphne was actually defending my dad's immoral behavior. She was on his side. This wasn't the first time I'd reached out to her regarding my concerns for our parents but this would certainly be the last.

It angered me that she did not see my way. I get that Dad is unhappy but he made a commitment. Our mother is honoring it although she also isn't the happiest camper. *Why couldn't he?*

"Look, I don't care what you say. It's wrong and mom needs to know!"

"No, Morgan. She doesn't. Stay out of it or someone could get hurt. Seriously," she looked at me sternly.

"Okay, fine," I agreed. "But she's gonna find out on her own sooner or later."

"Exactly, and you won't want to be in the middle. I've seen this happen to some of my friends and they all realized there's nothing they can do about their parents' actions. All you can do is love both your parents for loving you. Never mind the drama."

I was pretty sure my sister knew what she was talking about. She had seen and heard about experiences like this from her friends. But for me, it was brand new. This is the kind of stuff that rips families and lives apart.

Until now, I thought I was lucky to be living in a home filled with bliss. I thought my parents were exceptional for keeping peace and showing love. But the truth lie before me, and I was hurt to my core.

I even felt a tinge of guilt for keeping such a secret from my mom. She and I had a thick bond and on this very day, I could feel it weakening.

I did not want to betray my dad. I wanted to trust my sister. And I did not want to bring worry to my mom. So I did what was best for everyone and left them all alone.

Dear Diary,   *Wednesday July 16th*

After the scandal I witnessed between my father and that lady, I could hardly enjoy my family vacation anymore.

The waterpark we went to today was an absolute wash. The weather was gloomy. There was a trickle of rain. No one displayed signs of having any genuine fun. The secrets and lies that lingered amongst us were destroying our time.

Heading back to the resort was awkward. There was no casual conversation, no laughs, no closeness. I was resentful of my sister for making me promise to keep my mouth shut. I was growing hate toward my father for his infidelity. I felt sorry for my mother who struggled with weight issues just as I always had. And I was disappointed in myself for not having solutions.

Surely, there was something I could do to take my mind off all this mess.

So, I waited a few long hours until midnight. In just a few moments, I was scheduled to meet up with Jay down in the lobby by the snack bar.

I wasn't too sure what would result from our meeting this time, but I had to be prepared for anything.

I showered for hours. I got dressed in a slimming romper and sprayed on a most delightful fragrance.

My sister who was already laying in her hotel bed questioned my intentions. "Where do you think you're going?" she asked with a sleepy side eye.

I wasn't sure if I should share. But if there was anyone to tell, it would have to be her.

"Well, I was so caught up with mom and dad's drama so I forgot to tell you..."

"Sounds juicy! Tell me what?!" she sat up in her bed eagerly.

"I found the missing piece to the pool party puzzle."

"What do you mean," she asked.

"The guy."

"The guy you *did* it with?"

"Yup, that's the one."

"Wow, my prayers worked fast."

"Don't tell me you brought God into this mess."

"I just asked that you found this predator before I did. Because I wouldn't be able to control my actions if I ever met him."

I had to fill her in on what I had learned.

"Well, he's not exactly the predator we thought he was..." I started. "He's actually kinda cool."

"Oh boy, what do you mean?"

"He's just another underclassman who got hazed at my expense."

"That doesn't make sense," she sat there puzzled. "How could he make a move on you without getting your consent?"

I recalled a bit of a piece from that night. I remember walking into the pool house hot and ready to receive the man of my affection. I did not reject his touches nor his kisses. I even gave him a few of my own.

Walking into the bedroom, it was darker than the night. I

was grateful my every flaw wouldn't be exposed amongst the blackness. Music blared though every surrounding speaker. I moved to the rhythm of the bass. I guided his hands to the most pleasurable parts of my body. I enjoyed the moment.

But there was no way I could replay those memories for my younger sister.

"It's high school stuff. You *wouldn't* understand!" I exclaimed.

"And so you're gonna meet with him again? Doesn't sound like the greatest idea."

"Neither does sitting around here. So I'm out sis'. Don't wait up and don't let mom and dad know I was out."

"Mom and dad? As if they can pull away from their own shenanigans long enough to notice what we're up to."

"True, true. Well, in any case... conjure up a good lie for me. Thanks!"

She shrugged her shoulders and rolled back into her cocoon. "I didn't hear that. I'm asleep."

So I crept right out to meet up with him.

Dear Diary,   *Wednesday July 16th*

Jay and I chatted for hours. We learned more and more about each other.

He was on the junior basketball team with a few of the jerks I had known to be trouble. But Jay seemed different.

He was extremely straightforward. He was honest. He was open. He made me admit things to him that I hadn't even admitted to myself. And so I began to trust him.

"I was so focused on my insecurities that day, I don't even remember the good times..." I shared.

"We all have insecurities, especially athletes. There's a lot of pressure to be the strongest, the fastest, the best. But I'm learning to just enjoy what I do. Forget everything and everybody else," he affirmed.

"Yea, you're right. I think way too much about what others think of me sometimes."

"And what do *you* think of you, right now?" he asked.

"I think I'm cute... and cool. I love to eat and I love to dance."

"That's what's up. I think the same about you. And I love the same things as you," he said with a smile. "Let's head out of here and find a place we can get down with some tunes."

"I've been here for weeks, so believe me when I say, there's nothing for teenagers to do at this hour. We can't go to the casino, the lounge, the clubs, nothing..."

"So, you wanna come back to my room?" he suggested.

It was the only place we could go to extend the wonderful time we were having. It's where I wanted to be anyhow. I wanted him alone again. I was more than ready to relive the intimate moment we shared in the past. This time, I would be well aware and in control.

"I thought you'd never ask!" I got up with no hesitation. "Let's go."

In his room, I felt extremely comfortable. The room was

almost identical to mine, except he had one queen size bed instead of two.

His clothing was neatly hanging from hangers in his closet and shoes laid out in a row against the closet wall. He had a few magazines laying on the night table as well. The room was filled with a very masculine aroma of soap. His colognes were placed carefully on the bathroom counter.

"You're very neat, I see."

"And you're very observant, I observe," he replied.

"Yea, it's not often I step into another guy's room. I expected to see boxers all over and for the room to smell like feet."

"Not I," he said. "Cleanliness is next to Godliness and that might be as close as I can get." We laughed.

"Where those tunes at?" I asked, sitting on the edge of his bed.

"I got it all right here," he pulled out his Bluetooth speaker from a drawer and hooked up the tunes quick.

He took my hand and pulled me up to dance. He put his other hand around my body.

"Do you remember me holding your waist this way?" he asked.

"Nope, not at all." I normally would have been so ashamed for a fit dude like himself to place his hands on my love handles. But Jay made me feel at ease.

"I enjoyed the way you moved with me," he said. "And I'm enjoying it now."

I couldn't help but blush.

"What else did you like?" I asked.

"It's better I show you than tell you," he looked into my eyes and kissed me gently. I certainly didn't remember anything as mountain moving than that ever before in my life. I had never even kissed a guy before!

It was magical! The comfort of his arms, the softness of his bed, and the lure of the music put me in a feel good mood.

I lost consciousness of my body image issues. I was distracted by the intimate feelings and confidence of this tender loving dude. It was all too good to be true.

I pondered in silence, *could this be love?*

Dear Diary,   *Thursday July 17th*

I spent the entire day hanging out with Jay. We ordered room service, watched movies and went down to the game room. He was a cool brother.

I had to get back to my own room by dinnertime though. My family had reservations to eat at 7 o'clock.

When I returned to our floor and walked into our room, my sister was not at all getting prepared for dinner.

The look on her face told it all. Then, my mother walked out of our bathroom with tears in her eyes.

"I have to leave your father," she stated through sobs.

"No way, Mom. Why?" I ran over to comfort her. But I knew good and well there were several reasons.

"He's been cheating on me, girls. Different women, in different places." She sat on Daphne's bed. As strong as she was, this emotional tear at her heart must be weakening.

"How do you know?" I asked.

"I caught him red-handed, honey. He left the room late last night and I followed him. Long story short, I was looking for the truth and I got it. He doesn't love me anymore. Lord only knows what he's looking for out there but it's not me."

She put her head in her hands to cover her face. Daphne and I kneeled over her to pour our love into our mother.

Daphne offers words of comfort. "We love you, Mom. Always and forever."

"I know, girls. I love you too," she said resting her hands on our ours.

"Dinner would make us all feel a lot better. You guys wanna get going?" I asked. I was starving.

"Well, I can't eat," my mother replied. That was a first. "And I'm a mess. I can't go anywhere feeling this way."

"I could use dinner myself but I'm not leaving you right now," Daphne said.

"I'll get you guys something and we'll eat right here in the room," I resolved.

And so I left to get my mother a bowl of frozen yogurt topped with fruits and nuts. I thought it would be soothing and healthy. And for myself and Daphne, Thai food complete with white rice, spicy sauce, broccoli, and sheared beef.

It had been a very long time since we had any kind of bonding between the 3 of us. Daphne was always out killing kids on the court, me staying afterschool trying to save my spot on the squad, and Mom tending to my ungrateful father.

This moment was long awaited. The circumstances were

unfortunate. But it felt awesome being in the comfort of the 2 people I cared about more than anyone in the entire world.

Mom tore through that frozen yogurt in just a few minutes. We managed to get some smiles out of her and even a laugh. I assured my mother everything would be okay and God would make everything work in her favor. That would certainly put her at ease.

"Yes, Morgan, you are right. Can you pray with me?"

I reached out my hand to touch hers in agreement. She began to call out to the heavens, "I need your guidance, Lord. I feel broken and abused. Please take away this pain. Make me, my family, and my marriage anew. Amen."

As she concluded, she jumped up abruptly and ran to the bathroom. We followed closely behind. Mom had purged every bit of her delicious yogurt.

"I told you my stomach couldn't take it," she said. "I just need rest." So she cleaned up and went to lie down on my bed. The moment became tragic. I knew then and there that our lives would never be the same.

VOLUME 10: PLUS SIZE

Dear Diary,   *Friday July 18th*

I couldn't face my father today. I felt like I'd be betraying my mom.

She decided she'd had enough of my father's mess. She was ready to leave him and this island behind.

After breakfast, she had booked herself a "stomach treatment" of some sort as a final excursion for our trip.

I couldn't believe she was considering doing such a thing. With all her apprehension about me doing it, I was surprised she even had it on her mind.

"Wait a minute, are you sure?" I asked.

"With my heart now broken, I have nothing left to fear. Besides, I cannot live the rest of a divorced life as a plus size woman."

"Mom, no one sees you that way," Daphne added.

"And Dad does not want a divorce," I affirmed.

"This is not about anyone else. For once, I need to do something for me," she said.

There was not much else to say. If a little nip and tuck was necessary to ease her broken heart, who were we to stand in my mother's way? Of all people, I could certainly understand her reasoning.

"Mom, I know why you want to do this. But I honestly think you are the epitome of perfection. The beauty I see in you goes beyond skin deep. If I were you, I wouldn't change a thing," I poured in my two cents.

"Aww, I love you girls!" She reached out her arms to hold us both in a tight embrace. "I receive every word you've said. But my mind's made up. I'm going through with this and all I ask is that you support me."

"We got you, mom," we said in unison.

We packed our bags and readied ourselves to leave the day after this procedure. I pondered, *if things go well, would this bring me closer to a procedure of my own?*

I didn't dare bring that topic up, though. This moment was all about my mom.

Dear Diary,   *Monday July 21ˢᵗ*

The morning of the procedure finally came.

We got up bright and early and ate a bit of breakfast sent by room service. We still had not seen my dad in days. My mother had went back to her room a few times to get her belongings and he was no where to be found.

What a lame, I thought. He had disappointed my family in the worst way. And now mommy was preparing for surgery in a foreign country and he wasn't going to be by her side. *Smh!*

She called for a car service to transport us to and from the medical facility just minutes outside the resort.

When we arrived, the building looked more like an abandoned home than a medical facility.

"Are you sure you're sure about this?" Daphne uttered upon our arrival.

"Girls, stop worrying for me. I have enough worry in me for the three of us," she said, holding both of our hands and squeezing it tightly.

"Okie, dokie," I hopped out. "Let's do this then."

As we sat with the attending physician before the operation, I grew more and more afraid by the minute. The doctor rushed through the risks of getting liposuction and a tummy tuck at my mothers age. She stated the many precautions that were necessary following the procedure but had nothing to offer us in writing. She had no paperwork on my mother's past medical history present. And she accepted the balance of payment by hand.

All of these red flags should have been enough to send us home, but my mother was determined to leave there a skinnier woman. Nothing we said now could change her mind.

So we stayed there by her side and helped her into the patients robe. We watched as they pricked around her arm to find a vein to insert the IV. They stabbed her in the wrong place then had to bandage her up. No one seemed professional enough to take on this operation. Many things were not right.

Still, my mother disappeared into a small surgical room while Daphne and I waited outside the door.

Just as I was about to utter a prayer of protection, one of the medical assistants approached us.

"So!" she begun with a burst of energy. "Do either of you beautiful girls needs any work done while you're here in paradise?"

Daphne and I looked at each other. She knew what I was thinking. Therefore, she shook her head "no" for the both of us.

"Your mother will be under the knife for another few hours. We can hook you up with a boob job, a lift, lip injections, tummy tuck, face lift, butt lift..." her list went on and on. "You will never get these prices in your country, believe me."

"A butt lift?" Daphne said looking over her shoulder and at her behind. "Not a bad idea."

I laughed at her, "Girl, stop. You better never take a knife to your perfectly sculpted body." She had never showed any sign of insecurity so I couldn't let her start now.

"I won't if you don't!' she replied.

That was a fair enough deal but I didn't admit it out loud.

"Whatever," I said, rolling my eyes. She couldn't possibly understand the reasons I had for needing a change. This place certainly wouldn't help me make a case of it either.

"We're good, then," she responded to the medical assistant.

"Suit yourself," she said, flipping her luxurious extensions and turning away. "Let me know when you change your mind."

I thought about how simple and easy it would be to do the work right then and there. My parents wouldn't even know!

By the time their credit card bill came in the mail, I would be at my goal size and loving it. There would be nothing they could do but pay it.

On the other hand, we promised to support my mom. She may need lots of help these first few days of recovery. I can't take this moment away from her after all she's been through. And we have to get on a plane too...? I may be determined but I am not selfish.

Daphne and I sat anxiously awaiting our mothers return. But when the door opened, the doctor came out alone.

"There have been some complications," he said.

"What do you mean?" I stood up to ask.

"Her heart rate went up. Way up."

"What is that supposed to mean?" Daphne now stood up with concern.

"She's having some sort of cardiac distress. We need to get her to the nearest hospital," the doctor admitted.

"What?!" I couldn't believe what I was hearing. "Get her there, then!"

"We are not responsible for transportation, ma'am. You would have to call for your own ambulance."

"You haven't already called?!" I yelled.

This was getting more and more suspect by the moment. Daphne and I were panicking like crazy.

"I'll get the car," my sister said.

"Can I use your phone to call an ambulance?" I asked the doctor.

"You can try dialing out. Hopefully, you get through," he spoke so casually.

This was the scariest moment of my life. My mother's life was not to be reckoned with. And these people were being too passive about such a major health concern.

Luckily, I was able to reach the ambulance. They hurriedly made their way over to the hell house we were in. They got her off the operating table where I got a glimpse of her.

Her eyes were wide open but so was her mouth. She was frozen into a position of distress indeed. *Was she even breathing?*

"Mom, are you alright?" I got as close as I could to gain some clarity on my mother's condition but still, I couldn't tell. So I let the paramedics do their job.

They wouldn't let Daphne or I accompany our mother on the ambulance since we were both underage. Instead, we followed closely behind in our car service.

It was a bumpy and traumatic ride. Daphne and I sat in silence fearing the unknown. She was busy banging on the seats while I was knocking my head on the window glass. This was an unsettling experience.

When we arrived at the hospital, the nightmare unfolded as the attending doctor pronounced our mother dead on arrival.

You could have just killed us both right then and there too.

VOLUME 11: DOCTOR'S ORDERS

Dear Diary,   *Tuesday July 22nd*

We searched profusely for my dad when we returned to the resort. He didn't return to the room until early this morning.

Apparently he had heard the awful, life shattering news.

We had already cried our eyes out within the past few hours. The pain turned to contempt upon laying eyes on our father.

"Mommy basically died of a broken heart," Daphne wasted no time pouring the guilt on him.

"Yeah, she never had any heart problems before all this mess."

"Well, it wouldn't be fair of me to keep this from you any further... but your mother had a heart attack this time last year. She knew her lifestyle had to change for her health to improve. The doctor's orders were to cut down on meats and oils. She was supposed to start working out too. Her health was in a terrible place. I am shocked she would even consider seeing a surgeon without her cardiologist's approval."

"Are you blaming her for this?" I was getting angry.

"No, he's saying Mom knew this could happen," Daphne stated, deep in thought.

"And that's how badly you hurt her, Dad." I understood what this all meant but I wasn't letting him off the hook so easily. "She choose not to live with the pain you caused. So she chose death instead." I sat down and let a new stream of tears pour down my face.

"I'm sorry you girls feel that way. I never would have let this happen if I was aware of it."

"Well, that's what happens when you go chasing after other women, Dad. You become less aware of what's happening right in your own home, right under your nose." Daphne was giving it to him straight.

"We will sue the facility you guys went to," was all he could say. "And I promise you, we will win."

"Let's hope this is a promise you'll keep," I replied. I knew deeply, I could no longer trust my father. I was ready to get on the plane with Daphne as scheduled and get away from this awful island. Nothing good came from this trip anyway.

I only had an hour before Daphne and I had to leave to catch our flight. My dad was staying behind to handle to legalities of this unfortunate occurrence. We had to get home and out of that awful space.

I thought about the little bit of peace and pleasure I'd experienced on this trip being with Jay. I had to find him to express my gratitude.

I needed one more lasting memory of those awesome times.

So I dialed him room number and luckily he was there. I stepped inside his room and immediately broke down in tears.

"My mother died!" I screamed out to him. He was stunned and speechless.

All he could do to console me was surround his muscular

arms around my waist. "I'm sorry, Morgan. Let Jay make you feel a little better."

And that he did. He took my clothes off quickly and wasted no time arousing me with his hands.

In just minutes, he had climbed on top and helped me forget my troubles. I whispered in his ear, "Thank you. I feel a lot better."

"Anytime, bae."

I got up and started getting dressed. "I have to head back home today. My sister and I are catching a flight in just a few hours. I'll see you when you get back?" I confirmed.

"Yeah, no doubt," he said. "But I hope you're not thinking we're together or anything."

"Huh?"

"You seem a bit attached. Crying on my shoulder. Telling me your plans. All this was just a vacation fling."

"Uh, it was a pool house thing too, remember?"

"Yeah, but do you really count that? You thought I was someone else. You can't expect me to be your boo thing all of a sudden."

"I never said you were my boo thing!" Jay was starting to get out of line.

"Well I can tell that you're feelin' the kid. I think you should know that you're not really my type."

"Oh my gee! You are every bit the jerk I thought you were from the beginning!" I was very clear that this guy was a perverted user. It was sickening how quickly guys turn on their charm to get what they want. This guy had fooled me twice but never again.

I had gotten what I wanted from him anyhow. A fantasy to remember. Now I needed to get home to my reality. This place was no paradise to me, it was an absolute abyss. I needed out.

Dear Diary,   *Wednesday July 23rd*

The plane ride home was torture. There were the most awful thoughts crowding my head. Life and love were not panning out for my family the way we deserved.

I lost my mother. I lost my father's trust. I lost my virginity. I lost my first lust.

Surely, I can focus on something more empowering... More enlightening... More hopeful...

I looked out the airplane window and saw just one little star shining super bright against the dark skies. It had to be my mother up there showing me her light.

Twinkle

Twinkle Twinkle, my Mother, my star
How I wonder why God took you so far
Up above I know you're with the most High
You're the brightest diamond shining in the sky
Listening to and loving me like you're still here
When the winds blows, I feel your presence there
Sprinkle sprinkle your tender care on me
Shine your bright light so that I can see
Take me out of this sunken place
Make this awful hurt erase
Shower me with your nourishing tears
Live in my heart where I hold you most dear

VOLUME 12: CONTROL ME

Dear Diary,   *Tuesday August 7th*

I was numb for days, weeks, even. I couldn't possibly find the proper words of contempt to transcribe. My sister hasn't played a tennis match, nor has she even trained or practiced since it happened.

I haven't eaten. I haven't slept. I haven't been to the gym.

My dad decided to hire a housekeeper to take care of matters in the home. No one had washed a dish nor swept a floor since our return home.

Being in the house was depressing. My mother's absence left such a void in our lives and our hearts. Nothing could repair this throbbing pain. I mourned for her daily.

Today was the hardest of all, the funeral.

I went through all the motions. I greeted family and friends, I accepted hugs, and I shared the delicate words of my poem, *Twinkle*. But I couldn't eat anything from the bountiful baskets of goodies our guests prepared for us.

Nothing hurt like the image of my mother's body being lowered into the ground. This was the final goodbye but my soul could not let go.

I dreamt that my mother lay with me tonight. I was at ease as she put her loving hands on my face. She wanted me to know that although she was not there, she was not very far.

I chose not to believe that my mother was gone. So on this night, I finally got some peaceful rest.

Dear Diary,   *Friday August 10th*

I began to eat again. My new reality of constant despair had set in. So I finally opened my mouth to eat and the experience was endless. I couldn't stop.

By 8pm yesterday evening, I had thrown up 3 times. My dad did not deem it healthy.

His apparent guilt must have made him force me into a doctor's office today.

As Dr. Tremble took my vitals, I sat there impatiently waiting for her to speak.

"What seems to be troubling your stomach, young lady?"

"I lost my mother," I replied to the doctor. "Nothing I put in my body can fill that void."

"I completely understand, Morgan. But while she's gone in the physical form, she is with you in spirit."

"I know she's in my dreams but she's not right here."

"What have you been eating?" she asked.

"Who knows? Who cares? Nothing stays down anyway," I replied dryly.

"I care. And it matters because I want to make sure you're getting the nourishment your body needs."

"My body needs my mother right here next to me!" I raised my voice to respond. "Can you heal my loneliness?!"

"Well, I can make a recommendation to see a grief counselor. I'm sure she can help. But I also need to make sure you are consuming your vitamins and minerals daily. I will have to send a nutritionist to visit your home. Be open to the suggestions she gives you."

"Okay, yea sure." I was wholly disinterested in anything she had to say. Besides, all this under eating, binge eating, and purging was a huge contribution my weight loss efforts. I wasn't complaining one bit about that!

"And while you're here, I will be taking some blood and urine."

What's new? I thought.

Dear Diary,   Saturday August 11th

It was time for me to snap out of darkness. I could no longer allow this pain to control me. My mother would never have wanted me to spiral any further downward.

Mom would have told me to get up, get out, and go do something. I had to live up to her honor.

I needed comfort badly and no one in this empty hearted home could provide it for me.

I knew for sure that Troy would not hear from me after our last encounter. He thought I played him out badly.

I needed to see him though. I had to talk to him. He needed to know the truth. I'm sure if he gave me a moment to speak, he would feel my pain. He would empathize with these ill feelings I'd been harboring inside.

All I could think was to pay him a visit at Push Fitness. I was tricked and hurt just as badly as he was at the pool party. I needed to finally explain.

I pulled up to the fitness facility on my bike. A huge sign stood at the front.

"Keep pushing." it read in bold text. *What a powerful catchphrase*, I thought.

That alone gave me the courage to take a step off of my

bike and walk into the building.

Maybe Troy would hear me out if that's the kind of energy he's surrounded by.

Inside the state of the art facility, I was impressed by the organized rooms filled with machines and equipment. It was a whole new world to me.

I was intrigued by the spin and cardio dance classes that were in session.

Push Fitness was much more developed than our school's fitness center. Its clientele were serious and in shape. Working out was an extremely focused lifestyle. I didn't think I'd ever fit in.

"Can I help you?" a receptionist asked me as I stood there in amazement.

"Yes," I stammered out. "I'd like to find out about training sessions with Troy..."

"Troy's sessions are full today," she scanned through a document on the computer screen and then scanned my body with her eyes. "How about a cardio class?"

"I'm open to that," I figured a cardio class would definitely get me geared up for another cheerleading season. "But I still want to see Troy in action."

"Okay, sure. One of our tour guides will show you around until his class begins. Do you want to pay for your cardio session now?"

I handed her twenty bucks and awaited my tour. If Troy had even a moment of time to give me, I would gladly apologize to him for what happened at the pool party.

When the tour guide led me past the Olympic sized pool, up the stairs, and past the basketball courts, I was astonished to see Troy standing in the doorway of a private exercise room. His physique was more toned than ever before. His hair was cleanly shaven. My attraction for him grew.

"Morgan?"

"Hi, Troy," I spoke as assertively as I could. "I've had a long summer but it's been pretty lonely without you."

"I can only imagine what you've been up to since the last time I saw you..."

He was already giving me the guilt trip. I only hoped he'd hear me out.

"Well certainly nothing you're thinking... In fact, I spent most of it out of the country and had an unfortunate, untimely death in my family." I lowered my head reflecting back on the pain I'd encountered these past few weeks. "It has been rough so I needed to talk to a friend."

"I'm sorry to hear that Morgan. And you know I'm here for you," he offered his condolences then lifted his wrist to check the time. "However, now is not a good time or place."

"I figured as much. I just came to see you in action," I lightened the mood. "Apparently your sessions are too packed to fit little ole me!"

"Nah, couldn't be!" he was surprised. "I'll get you in."

"No, it's okay. I already paid for a cardio class. I need some private time with you anyway," I teased.

"Sounds good to me. I'll hit you up later then." I handed him a slip of paper with my home number and email on it. I couldn't wait to speak to him later.

VOLUME 13: VIOLATE ME

Dear Diary,   *Sunday August 12th*

Troy never called me that night. I was obsessively checking my emails to see if he'd at least dropped a line, and to no prevail.

I was beating myself up inside trying to understand whether I'd ruined our relationship forever. *Did he think I was easy? Could he have heard about my encounters with Jay? Surely his twin brother would tell him if he only knew. Did I come off desperate at his job yesterday? Does he have a new, more special girl in his life? Am I no longer important to him? Will we at least be friends again?*

I sobbed myself to sleep that night. The pain in my heart was growing into a sick cancer. I could not escape my mistakes so I fell asleep in defeat.

Dear Diary,   *Monday August 13th*

I needed my space. I couldn't be around anyone. I couldn't speak. I couldn't laugh. And I could no longer cry.

I felt empty inside, like there was nothing in my soul to pour out.

So when my dad knocked on my door to offer me dinner, I ignored him. And when he slowly tried opening the door to peek in, I ran to the door full speed to slam it closed.

"How dare you violate me like that?" I yelled out at him. "I could be naked."

I still had so much disdain for my dad. I didn't speak to him much, he wasn't home very often, and we had not had one meal as a family since that awful trip.

"I was just coming to check on you, darling. It's time for us to talk."

"Not right now," I sat against my side of the door, weakened by my emotions.

"I understand. But please tell me when."

"Just not right now," I replied. I wasn't ready to let him into my life again. I wanted to create the distance he must be feeling. I need him to feel the guilt, the pain, and the suffering that the rest of us have felt. Not that it would ease my heartbreak but at least he should know where my heart is- still with mom.

Dear Diary,   Tuesday August 14th

My heart continued to grow heavy with hate. I still hadn't heard from Troy. I hadn't spent any time with my friends. I even shut out my sister for supporting my dad.

The hate within me was getting real. There was only one thing my mother said could negate ever that- love.

She had always told me that God's love was greater than any man's and I should always seek Him first.

So I kneeled down at my bedside and sought him out.

Dear God, it's me Morgan

VOLUME 14: LOVE ME

Dear Diary,   *Sunday August 19th*

My prayers were answered! My heart had softened. I didn't wake up in such excruciating emotional pain today. So I continued to call out to Him.

Shine your light on me
Give me your love
Lord I need your mercy
Protect me like your favorite dove
Show me your power
Live throughout my soul
I kneel in your honor
Your very name makes me whole
Lead me to the Promise land
Guide my every step
Reveal your peace to me
Comfort me as I wept
Embrace me, oh God
Let every voice sing praises
Tell me you love me
Through my best and worst phases

Dear Diary,   *Monday August 20th*

I was over being lonely and subdued. I needed a friend. Someone who would open up and pour something good into my soul.

Just because Troy had given up on me, it didn't mean I had to be alone. It was time for me to return my friends' calls and visits. I needed someone to help me love again.

It was rare that I ever did this, but I called on Patricia. She certainly knew pain and could relate to the feeling of having an absent parent.

❀   ❀   ❀

I asked my dad to drop me over by Patricia's. He was eager to finally speak to me so he dropped everything he was doing to satisfy this favor.

On the way over to the home that Dr. Graham and Patricia reside, he attempted to offer a few more apologies.

"I cannot tell you enough how sorry I am for hurting this family," he began. "And I know you're tired of hearing it but I'll state it as many times as I have to until I have your forgiveness."

"Dad, I forgive you. *We* forgive you." I gave in to his plea. "So please don't let the guilt eat you up any longer. What's done is done and no one's blaming you for what happened to mom."

"I appreciate that honey. But I can't help feeling so very responsible. As the man of the house, I should have been protecting you all. Protecting her heart. Protecting our love."

He was right. He did have a major responsibility to our family and while he failed greatly at it, I had to maintain my forgiveness. I couldn't hold onto this contempt any longer.

Besides, this was the apology I was waiting for. This was the wholehearted truth I wanted him to admit. I needed to know that he was finally acknowledging his faults in this. Only then can we move toward positive changes.

"Well, dad, it's not too late to protect our love. Daphne and I are suffering and can use your support daily. With all the troubles we're experiencing, we hope you will be back by our side."

I didn't feel as though he was emotionally present for us during the final days or even months of my mother's life. He was always more consumed with work or with his external relationships that his attention seemed far off at a distance.

"Sweetheart, I never left and never will. I promise."

As we arrived to our destination, I thought to myself, *my dad is back.* I hadn't realized how much I missed having him involved in my life and experiences. It was seldom that he would drop his paperwork to pay me any mind. And here we were, sharing a car ride together.

He assured me that with my mother so far gone, he would never go that distance. It was all the strength I needed to spend the day venting to Patricia.

I popped up from my back seat and hugged him with all my strength.

"Love you, dad!" I said as I left the car excitedly.

"Call me when you're ready hon'."

"Thanks! Bye," I waved back at him with the most genuine smile I had on my face since our family vacation had begun.

I was learning to love again.

Dear Diary,   *Friday August 31ˢᵗ*

Having spent some quality time with Patricia, I was really learning the value of friendship. There was nothing like having an extension of your family to support you through such hardships.

It made me realize how important it was to check up on all my friends.

I had been so consumed by my own tragedy that I hadn't

stopped to consider how Tiffany's pregnancy was going, nor how Tammy has been coping with her absentee mother all these years.

It was time to round up the girls and bond again.

Today was Patricia's birthday and a better time than any other to round the crew up and have some fun.

We all met up at the skating rink in Hicksville. Apparently Patricia had this birthday ice cream tradition she wanted us all in on.

Dr. Graham came inside the seating area and placed a square cake filled with icing and edible décor on our table. The cake was exquisitely designed with purple and gold icing and had images of dancers and musical notes throughout. It was the most beautiful cake we had ever seen.

Patricia gushed over the cake. "Dr. Graham! You outdid yourself with this one. I never had an ice cream cake before. Heck, I've never even had a birthday cake but this gathering right here-" she looked around at all of us and started tearing up. "This one literally takes the cake... all of them!"

It was blissful witnessing the tears of joy streaming down Patricia's face. Having recently connected with her heart and soul, it was equally joyful for me to share in her moment.

Just as I had recently felt the comfort of her words when I poured out my pain onto her shoulders a few days ago, I received the love she expressed now.

We sang a few versions of "Happy Birthday", took a million selfies, and cut the cake. Dr. Graham bought us all milk shakes from the concession stand and pizza. She sat down to enjoy this birthday treat with us for a few minutes.

Her phone rang and before picking it up, she passed it to Patricia. "It's for you, Pat. It's your mother."

Again, Patricia lit up with glee. "Ma?" she answered. How have you been?" Patricia walked away from the group for a moment. She probably needed a little privacy to ask her mom some long awaited questions about her recovery. Upon her return, she breathed a huge sign of relief.

"Everything okay?" Tiffany asked.

"Yup, everything's okay," Patricia replied.

After a glance at her watch, Dr. Graham told us, "I have an appointment to run to. I'll be back to pick you girls up in two hours. Call me if you need me before then."

"Sounds good," Patricia agreed. "Now let the celebrations really begin!"

"Party safe," Dr. Graham got up to say. She kissed Patricia on the forehead and was on her way.

I felt a tinge of emptiness when I witnessed that interaction between my friend and her new guardian. I realized in that moment that I would never have my mother to kiss me so adoringly on the forehead like that ever again.

It was great timing and an accurate mind reading when Tammy opened her mouth to say what I'd been feeling.

"You're damn sure lucky to have *her*!"

"What do you mean?" Patricia said, stuffing her face with pizza.

"I'm saying, here we are- Morgan and I- without even one mother in our lives. And you get two! That's pretty cool."

"I can't possibly tell you what it's like to be completely without a mother figure but I can tell you I know how it feels to be parentless. Y'all already know what my life was like for many years dealing with my mother and her abuse... Not knowing my dad was an emptiness you'd never *ever* want to encounter..."

"Well, newsflash honey!" Tammy interjected. "That's what we're feeling now and forever more."

"Don't wish that feeling on your forever," Tiffany said. "You will heal from it at some point."

"Doubt it," I said. "My mother is never coming back. How will the loneliness I feel ever heal?"

"You know," Tammy adds. "I would be at a much higher level at peace if I knew my mother had passed away. But knowing she's out there somewhere just not caring about me is so much worse. She actually has a choice and she *chose* to forget all about me." She shook her head with dismay.

"I don't think any of us should compare," Patricia said. "We all know what abandonment feels like. We can rest assure that we got each others back no matter how awful that feeling gets us feeling."

"You're right," Tiffany joked. "So with my baby daddy hardly showing me any attention now, can I depend on all of you to help me love this child?"

"Come on, girl! You already know it!"

We all laughed as we began clearing up our table. We were ready to roll around the crowded rink. The disco ball was spinning and the dj's music was blaring.

"You guys go ahead," Tiffany urged us. "I can't risk falling on my butt or this belly. I'll sit here and keep an eye on your belongings..."

While out on the rink, Patricia caught up to me to follow up on our latest conversation. I opened up to her about my family vacation from hell and the untold story of Jay and my interaction from the pool party onto the island of death and disappointment.

"So, what's up?" she asked. "Has Troy called you back yet?"

"No ma'am. I think he's over me. The moment has passed for us."

"That can't be the case," she replied. "I saw the way he looked at you at the end of the school year. I even noticed how he treated you at the pool party. That guy's got it bad for you girl."

"All of that was before I did the unthinkable," I explained. "He probably has a whole new view of me now."

"Don't think that way for another minute! The only thing he could possibly think of you is the truth. That you want him and always have."

"If only things were so simple for us..."

"What do you mean? It *is* that simple."

"No," I had to break it down for her. "Things may be simple for you because you're cute and skinny. But for Troy and I, we face a whole other battle... We get teased and ridiculed daily. We have to work harder just to get a spot on our favorite teams and bust our tails trying to maintain it. People talk crap about us so much we barely know who to trust. And at the end of the day, we can't receive the love we deserve because we struggle trying to love ourselves."

"Okay, whoa! You really think *I* have it any easier?" Patricia started. "All my life, I have had to fight the same battles. Low self esteem, low self worth, abandonment, loneliness, and not to mention- domestic and street violence. People will do some evil things to anyone they feel is weaker. I've been on the harsh end of that rude awakening for most of my life. The only way you overcome the hate is to defend yourself by showing love. And I think you know that, Morgan."

"I know, I know. My mother shared that secret with me... but I don't believe it always applies."

"Try it. Give love another chance. Self love. Platonic love. Family love. Even hater love. When I finally met my dad this spring, he told me to ignore all the bad I had going on and focus on all the good. It has seriously changed my life."

"Like I said, I wish things were so simple for me," I skated away from her before tears could well up in my eyes.

I wanted to believe her but every horrible thing that could happen to me this summer, actually had. It was a sweet treat to be out with my friends today but the bitter truth was that by nighttime, I would be back home living amidst my pain.

There was no escape for me. I tried to drown my sorrows into the music by rocking to every fast paced beat. Besides, I couldn't pass up the opportunity to burn the additional calories I'd just consumed.

I tried to replay Patricia's words in my head. She certainly had a renewed spirit these past few months. Maybe her positive thinking had taken her far beyond her troubles. I wondered if this could ever work for me.

Ignore all the bad and focus on the good. Maybe I'll give it a try. There was no way I could live with this ongoing pain. I had to give her advice an honest try. I had to start from the basics. I had to learn to love me.

VOLUME 15: MISSING YOU

Dear Diary, *Sunday September 2nd*

My sister and I hadn't spent much time talking since we lost our mother. There was a silent hurt we both couldn't address. So we stayed as busy as we could in the midst of our grieving.

But I was missing something from our sisterhood and I had to find it.

Before I sought out my sister to speak, I kneeled down to reflect on a divine purpose.

Missing You

A beautiful beginning led to this bitter end
Joy erased from our hearts and we just cant pretend
A bond so strong quickly ripped away
One bad move opened this wedge of dismay
Our lives so different but share one broken touch
The loss of our mother is a harsh terrain that erupts
Because every time I step foot in this house
I feel hollow in this home with no one moving about
I cry out to you now, longing for your presence
Needing just one more person living at this residence
If not she, can it be you?
Hold my hand and let self love become two
Because I'm lost and I'm losing in everything I do
I'm drowning in sorrow 'cause I can't help missing you
Give me your strength, be by my side
Forget about death, let's jump on this joyride
Teach me how to rekindle our peace
Help us to live within each other's reach
Show me how to unconditionally love
We'll start from the bottom and climb to Him above

With a clear intention to reconnect with my sister, I found her watching a virtual reality horror movie in her room.

"What's up, Morgan?" she asked as I slipped through the door. Her eyes were fixated inside the VR lens. It was a wonder how she knew it was me.

"Absolutely nothing at all." I sat down to engage. "Missing you, that's all."

"I've only been one door away," she said sarcastically.

"Yeah, true. But it's been difficult for me to take even those simple steps."

"I get it." Daphne continued to watch her film.

"Well I just came to offer my support to you. I think things would be a lot easier if we took them on together. That's all.

Now, I had her attention. She took off the VR eyepiece and turned straight to me.

"It's about time you stepped back into reality, sis." The irony of that considering she had been indulging in her virtual world only seconds ago. "I was wondering when I'd have my sister back. I even prayed about it this morning."

"Here I am!" I reached out my arms to embrace her.

She backed away for a moment to ask, "I hope it's not too soon… but are you eating at all?"

"I'd say *overeating* at this point…" I had to shy away to admit the truth. Didn't want to share my purging habits on top of it either.

"Well at least that tells me you're back!" She high fived me as I reluctantly slapped back.

Was that a dig? I thought. But I quickly averted my thoughts to Patricia's last words. *Ignore the bad. Focus on the good.*

I pulled my sister in close to focus on the newfound feeling of togetherness. While I was worrying about my losses and my shortcomings, my sister was worrying about me. No winning match nor summer game could have cheered her up the way she was right now. She had missed me too. Flaws and all. *This was love.*

Dear Diary,   *Monday September 3rd*

Today was Labor Day! It was the final hooray before we had to start preparing for the return to school. So I pulled my sister out of her own depressive state, sitting in front of the VR screen, to take her to Troy's gym.

We always bonded with a little fitness, something we both needed for our own varied reasons. So we biked over to *Push Fitness* to redeem my cardio fitness class passes.

We had a blast. I came out of that room dripping with sweat. They had us working our tail feathers from every angle. The music was lit with an actual Disc jockey on the 1's and 2's within the space.

I was determined to meet my goal weight in a matter of days. I could do this everyday if it would help me do it. I only wished I had spent more time this summer getting into shape. I would've been much closer to my goal had I snapped out my depression sooner.

Nonetheless, I was on my way up and out of it. I was focusing on everything that is good so weight loss, friendships, family and self love would set me free. It didn't even bug me that I was in such close quarters to Troy and hadn't seen him. Nor did I stress that we hadn't had that heartfelt conversation I was longing for. I was determined to ignore all things that made me feel bad. I trusted God to put the pieces of my shattered heart back together. Everything else had started falling back into place.

Afterwards, Daphne and I went to the pool to cool off. As we dipped our toes into the calming water, we finally exhaled.

VOLUME 16: INCOMPLETE

Dear Diary,   Thursday September 6th

It was time to return back to school. With a newfound love for family and friends, I thought I could go about society with a little more ease.

With all my challenges this summer, the cheerleading squad seemed so trivial now that I've lost the most important piece of my heart and soul.

And when I walked in the school building, I continued to feel strangely incomplete.

Not having spoken to Troy in months then returning to the very location we met, gave me another round of painful loneliness.

During my lunch period, I walked slowly past the fitness center hoping to bump into him at the entrance or catch a glimpse of him doing his workout thing. But there was no trace of him anywhere.

It was only the first day of school and that feeling of emptiness was cascading back over me. I was longing for a simple conversation. I needed a chance to look him in the eye and apologize for everything I'd done to betray our friendship- unknowingly or not.

Thankfully, my girls were saving me a spot at their table in the cafeteria. I needed a serious distraction to get me through the rest of this day.

"What's on the menu?" I asked peeking into their lunch trays to see what mystery meat we'd be eating today.

"Tacos with beef," Tammy said.

"I could dig it," I said.

"Ain't you dieting?" Tiffany asked.

Looking at her big ole pregnant belly, I couldn't even take too much offense. "Girl, why you putting me on blast though?"

"I'm just trying to help."

"Whatever, summer's over. All of my unflattering angles will be hidden behind big shirts and baggy jeans again."

"You pregnant too?" Tiffany questioned me, sarcastically.

"No, silly," I hit her.

"We never know with you, Morgan. Coming all late to lunch like you're boo'd up again..." Tammy insinuated that I had a lunch meet up.

"Quite the contrary, girls." I haven't really opened up to the entire crew about Troy and my drama. "We haven't spoken in a while. I did go looking for him but no luck."

"Oh, so that's why you're gonna ruin your diet?" Tiffany continued to press the eating issue. "You're all in your feelings. *Cute.*"

This was truly the reason why I had been keeping my personal matters to myself lately. I couldn't handle the judgment. I had become too weak.

Patricia speaks up, "Can't a girl eat a real meal without all the mockery?"

That girl was becoming such a valuable part of the group, I must say.

"We're just looking out for *her*," Tammy replied. "She's about to get kicked off the squad. I'm just saying..."

Leave it to Tammy to continue to kick me when I'm down.

"Patricia probably wants her spot when she's gone!" Tiffany laughed.

"Not even," Patricia glared at her. "*Your* spot's already open."

"Ouch!" Tammy said bringing her hands to her mouth. "You girls are brutal."

"Look, y'all. I'm already having a hard day. If this banter is gonna continue, I'll sit somewhere else."

And so I left the table and went to get on the lunch line. As I walked away, I heard Tiffany utter her apologies.

It was easy to forgive her petty words. I had much bigger problems than that anyhow.

For instance, *would I get the taco today? Or should I head on over to the salad bar? Decisions, decisions...*

As I stood at the cafeteria crossroads, my desperate dream had come true. Someone had stepped close behind me and touched my shoulder.

"Hey Morg! You're trying to decide whether to 'stomach it or not to stomach it' aren't you? After all the good food I ate all summer long, I am definitely with you!"

It was Troy!

"Troy?" I turned to face him. "I was actually trying to decide *what* to eat because I'm most definitely hungr- never mind." I decided not to share my greed with anyone else. I should be the one asking the questions anyway.

"I'd say get a taco salad," he affirmed. I hadn't even thought about that. Tacos with all the good stuff except the meat. *Genius.*

But even his splendid idea wasn't enough to make me

forget we had unfinished business.

"Never mind that. What happened to you this summer? You never called me."

"Oh yea! I know. I put your number in my pocket that day and it got so sweaty I couldn't make out any of the numbers. I tried calling an assortment of numbers that weren't quite it. You wouldn't imagine how hard I tried..." he chuckled thinking back to it.

It was hard to believe he had even tried at all. All this time, I thought he was trying to play me out.

"You're lying," I stated.

"Not at all. I invited you to my gym for a reason. I waited *how* long to finally see you there, then that happened. There wasn't much I could do."

"Whatever," I gave him a hard time. "Let me get my food."

"I'll be sitting right there," he pointed to the closest table to the lunch line. "Waiting for you."

I nodded my head. I could totally dig it. We had just a few moments to talk before our next class. And a moment was all I needed. (;-)

Dear Diary,   *Friday September 7ᵗʰ*

Troy and my convo lasted longer than our lunch period. I ended up getting to my next class late and then continuing our chat afterschool. Today, he invited me to a juice bar nearby. He wanted to show me how he's been dieting and cleansing without compromising his meal schedule, flavor, or any nutrient intake.

The place was cozy and inviting. It was called, *Juice Vibes.* There was definitely a vibe when you enter the narrow space. Light music was playing, chairs and tables were spread throughout, and a soothing aroma filled the air.

There was a colorful menu of fruit packed drinks posted up on a board. It displayed all the ingredients within each luscious drink. You could order snacks and pastries such as nuts, chips, or wheat bread to complement any concoction. There were shakes, and acai bowls, and blended juices galore.

"What are you having?" Troy asked me.

"This isn't easy," I replied. "But I'll have the Lean Body Buttermilk." It was a soy milk shake with a peanut butter base and an assortment of fruits mixed in.

"Good choice," he agreed. "Ask for a sprinkle of cinnamon and you'll be in for an even bigger treat!"

I trusted Troy at this point. After speaking with him these past two days, we entered a new level of our friendship. I finally got to apologize for the things that went down at the pool party. He was as shocked as I was to learn that I'd been tricked into thinking I had him waiting in the pool house .

"Damn, that's crazy. So even my brother knew about this?"

"I don't want to start anything between you and your brother though, I just want you to know the truth," I said.

"Nah, it's all good. Me and my brother beef all the time. We just don't see things the same. He thinks all girls are whores. He's always trying to prove it to me like I live under a rock or something. But he was terribly mistaken about you and I'll have him know it."

It was a relief knowing that Troy had my back. Even some of my closest friends hadn't shown me that kind of loyalty. Just when I was feeling my lowest, Troy always saw me for the person I am inside and treated me exactly as I deserved. It was refreshing having someone who valued me in such a way and truly supports me on this journey.

Dear Diary,   *Friday September 14th*

Today was our first day meeting back with the cheerleaders. I was not as excited as I was anxious to see if I had satisfied the weight requirements to stay on the squad.

I had done everything in my weakest powers to get fit, get healthy, and get picked for another season. From cutting out carbs for a moment, eating without meat from time to time, working out on occasion, depressively under eating after my mother's death, and purging regularly; I was sure my weight loss efforts were not in vain.

"Morgan Thomas!" one of the new captains called out. It was time for my weigh in.

"You look *good*," she said as I stepped up. That was a already a good sign. There was a noticeable change in me.

"Thanks, Jana" I smiled.

After taking a few notes, she made a face of disappointment. Jana and I were cool since last year when she was a junior. Now that she was co-captain, there was no telling what new characteristics would come out of her. Or what awful truths she would discover about me.

"Dang girl, I was hoping you were good." *Uh oh*, I thought.

"I was hoping so too. What is it?" I asked.

"Well, the captains last year required you a ten pound weight loss... but you only lost five." She shook her head.

"That's pretty close, don't you think? If I work twice as hard, I'll get there in no time, I promise."
"That *is* true," Jana thought to herself, tapping the pen on

her head. "Okay, I can let you keep your spot on the squad..."

"Yes!" I pumped my fist with relief and excitement.

"Let me finish though," she continued. "You won't be able to perform until you lose it all. We have to take your uniform from you for now. We can't have anyone bursting out the seams on the dance floor."

"Wow," this was a little bittersweet. It was even a bit embarrassing. I couldn't be mad though. I hadn't met the expectations that were clearly set. Now I had to prove I could go all the way with my fitness plan.

I knew just who could help me get there.

"Sorry, girl. Captain's orders. Even I have to follow them." She shrugged.

Before I left to get on it, I had one more inquiry. "So what will I do on the squad while I'm benched?"

"Keep up," she said and she was gone on to the next. So I got up and began some serious cardio exercise. I had to take this weight loss a lot more seriously if I was ever going to perform with the squad again.

Dear Diary,   *Tuesday September 18th*

During cheerleading practice today, the girls were beginning auditions for the new freshmen. It was shameful for me having to sit there and watch. I had taken a few glimpse of the girls and guys lined up for auditions to possibly take my place. I couldn't fathom never having the chance to perform again.

After sizing up each young contender, I excused myself and went straight to the fitness center.

Troy wasn't there for a change. I believe he was on the field for the football team tryouts all week long. This exercise would not be easy without his guidance and motivation.

Who would help me set the machines? Catch me when I fall? Give me great food options after the workout? Walk me home? None of this came naturally for me.

After about twenty minutes on the cardio machine, I decided to go visit him at his tryouts. Surely, he would appreciate my support.

It was quite a coincidence though, that I would be getting sidelined this semester while he was getting his final shot on the team.

Out on the field, it was cool but sunny. The guys were finishing up their warm up and were resetting to break out into groups based on their positions. Troy had already told me he wanted to try for the quarterback position but it was extremely competitive. In efforts to better his chances, he went for the running back position instead.

As they were breaking, Troy noticed me sitting midway up on the bleachers. I waved flirtatiously and couldn't help but blush when I saw the corners of his lips curl up into a smile.

This dude was beginning to strike some heavy chords in my heart. I felt so proud and alive being there in support of him. Troy wasn't even my man, but I knew our friendship alone was worth my time and affections.

The players began doing drills such as mirror passes and figure eight footwork circles. It was pretty cool checking out how the athletes got prepared for their sport. Meanwhile, the cheer squad members were doing lunges and leg lifts as warm ups and drills.

I thought it was pretty cool how all physical activities had such a precise training regime. I'd recently caught a glimpse of a boxing match and noticed the repetitive movement styles. Even swimming had a synchrony that was artistic and astonishing. It all inspired me to dance. I thought about what Jana had said. *Keep up!* Were her last words to me.

In that moment, I got a really great idea! I could do more than just 'keep up' with the squad. While I'm on this break, I would do a lot more than that. There's only been one way I'd ever lost any weight anyhow, and that's been shaking my tail feather. Only one thing would make me feel complete again.

With the plan I had in mind, I may even earn my way back onto the performance team soon than later. I couldn't wait to share my thoughts with Troy.

Hopefully he would agree it was a valid concept so I could readily run with it. Especially since I'd probably need his help.

VOLUME 17: MONEY VS. POWER

Dear Diary,   *Thursday September 20th*

My dad had scheduled a family dinner with my sister and I tonight. We had to come home straight from school today to wash up.

I couldn't wait up for my friends today nor check for Troy during his football tryouts.

At home, Daphne had beat me to the bathroom.

"Dang, girl! What'd you do, run home?" I screamed from my side of the door.

"You know it!" she exclaimed.

"Well hurry up!" I screamed back.

I went downstairs to use the half bath restroom. While down there, I heard my dad speaking with someone. It sounded like a woman.

Rage filled my insides. I hoped this was not my dad's introduction to his new woman. I would not be able to get through dinner if so. I did not know if I could even show up.

Before heading back to my room, I crept up to the study and peeped in.

It was in fact a woman. She had a thick accent. They were sitting far apart though. Their interaction was very professional.

I listened in to see if I could catch a glimpse of their conversation.

"I'm sure the girls will be thrilled to have you here. You were highly recommended and I am certainly pleased thus far..."

I heard my dad say.

"Well the accommodations are quite pleasing to me as well," she winked at him.

"It seems we have both made good decisions. Let's hope the girls agree," he replied.

"Indeed," she said.

I couldn't quite tell what was going on. I crept away and remained patient to find out the truth at dinner.

As I was the last to join the group as dinner, my dad jumped up to pull out my chair for me.

"Good evening, guys," I greeted my family along with this strange woman.

"Hey, sis," Daphne acknowledged.

"Daphne has already met Miss Cindy. Miss Cindy, this is my eldest daughter, Morgan."

"Hey," I waved suspiciously.

"Great to meet you, Morgan. That's a beautiful outfit," she referred to my short sleeve sweater dress from Zara.

"Thanks," I said to her then turned to my dad. "Who is she, dad?"

"Great question, hon'." He seemed nervous to come out with the introduction. So weird. "Miss Cindy is our new housekeeper. She's a licensed nutritionist and is going to help us around the kitchen during the week."

"Cool," Daphne started. "It's been pretty deserted in here for quite a while."

It truly annoyed me that Daphne would say that. Of course

it's been deserted in the kitchen lately. It's where our mother spent most of her time. Why would anyone want to occupy this bare space? Her comment nearly brought me to tears. Mom was never coming back and our kitchen would always bring me dismay.

"It's time we start filling the house with some good energy," dad said. "Cindy's prepared a meal for us all to get that energy moving."

"Yes I did!" Miss Cindy pops up and returns to the table with a tray. "Here is your first course- balsamic salad with bacon crumbs. Bon appetit!" She served us each a small plate with greens and a touch of dressing. The bacon bites were genius because it added the perfect pop of flavor to top off a deliciously, fresh salad.

"Delish!" my sister exclaimed, ravished at every bite.

I had to agree but I didn't do so out loud. I waited for the main course to come forth.

It was a plate of lemon pepper chicken with brown rice. Peas and carrots on the side. *Brown rice? Yuck!* I thought. That certainly ruined the food fantasy I was anticipating.

I tried to be polite as I picked around my plate.

"So dad, how'd you meet Miss Cindy?" I jumped right to it.

"Well, your doctor recommended a few food specialists and so did some of my friends. I've been doing interviews for weeks and..." he looked over at this strange lady. "Miss Cindy was the best I could find."

"Oh really? Don't you think we would've liked to be a part of the interview process?" I replied.

"Well, yes. Sure and you've met her now. I hope you can give your final word of approval."

"So if we don't like her, you'll kick her to the curb?" I concluded.

"Not with that kind of disrespect," my dad answered, looking toward Miss Cindy hoping I hadn't intimidated her.

I crossed my arms over my chest. I knew I was being a brat but I was annoyed by this woman's presence. My dad was overly impressed by her when her meal preparation wasn't even all that.

Apparently, Daphne disagreed. "Well, I give you and this meal two thumbs up!" she stated.

"Oh, whatever," I hissed under my breath.

"Seems like you guys are ready for dessert," she continued her servitude.

"We certainly are," my dad answered.

As she returned to the table, she placed a slice of carrot cake in front of each one of us. It was soft inside and lightly sweetened. I'm not usually a fan of carrot cake but I was impressed by this concoction. I let out a sigh of delight as I completed the last bite.

"Not bad," I stated. "What else do you have up your sleeve?"

"Well, Miss Cindy will be doing some light housework during the week so she will stay in the guestroom whenever necessary. Please get to know her as she will be sharing lots of time with the family."

"Oh, so she's like... living here now?" Daphne asked.

"Only when necessary," my father repeated.

I knew there was something deeper going on than what was in those pots. I felt a bit betrayed by my dad, but I decided not to let those feelings eat me up inside.

I had forgiven my father for all that went wrong with our family. I guess this was his way of trying to make things right. None of us had been eating very well lately. We hadn't even been seeing each other. I wish our first family meal together could have just been *family*, but I had to let go of the pain I felt and trust my father to take control.

I lightened up a little so everyone could enjoy this dinner. It wasn't perfect but it was a bit of fresh energy.

"This was great, dad," I acknowledged his efforts as I readied myself to escape the dinner table. "Thanks, Miss Cindy. I'd like to excuse myself now."

"Very well," my dad replied. "I hope you're headed straight for those books!"

"No doubt, dad," I got up and took my dishes with me.

"I'll handle those for you this evening," Miss Cindy took the plates out of my hands.

"Cool, thanks," I said, astonished. We never had a housekeeper before so clearing our own tables was never an option. It was imperative.

Once locked away in my room, I lie down on my bed and drowned myself in my thoughts.

Life was certainly different for me sophomore year than it was freshman year. My mother gone, my virginity taken, cheerleading on hiatus, an odd crush, a new friend, a strange houseguest, a few excess pounds, and a genius idea. Of all the hardships I could have counted, I realized then and there how great a role my weight loss would play in creating a better life for myself.

I needed to get on it. ASAP!

Dear Diary,   **Friday September 21ˢᵗ**

Troy made the football team! I was more excited for him than he was! He expressed how surreal it was or him. He had worked hard and long for years to be able to accomplish such a huge goal. He was determined to make every moment worth it.

Meanwhile, I had easily made the squad last year with the help of my crew. But even they couldn't pull me up from my current fall. It was totally up to me.

So as Troy and I walked home from school today, I anxiously shared my genius idea with him. This was gonna fix my problems by giving me great motivation to workout and to stay relevant on the squad.

"All I need is a little bit of your help," I requested of Troy. "What do you say?"

"It sounds awesome, Morgan. But I'll be at football practice just about everyday. There's not much I can do to help."

"Wow, true. I hadn't thought about that. Well maybe you can create some workout activities for me. Just like write them out.."

"I'll do whatever I can for you, you already know that. But my priorities have slightly changed, along with my schedule and my goals. Now I have to focus on staying on the team. And I'm looking at scholarships for college too..."

It was ironic how this year I'd been benched while Troy was finally getting the play he deserved. I had to work hard to get back my name and reputation as a cheerleader. That was the only way I could keep up with him.

"I get it," I said hanging my head down with defeat.

Troy had hit the big leagues. His confidence and social status had instantly plummeted. Never mind little ole me still trying to catch up with people in the fitness center. Before long, he won't even want to hang with me at all.

When was I going to get my body right? It was time for me to get all the way focused.

Dear Diary,   *Monday September 24th*

I had already been having mixed feelings about our new housekeeper and cook. She was very young, extremely thin, she was British, and she could cook *almost* as good as my mom.

Her skills could *never* measure up but it was cute that she tried.

Her vibes were weird. It always seemed like she was trying to get a little to close.

It was starting to get uncomfortable that she would often cook and clean for us, then join us for family dinners. She began to make casual conversation with us even pressed me a bit for feedback about tonight's feast.

"How did you like the eggplant parmesan tonight, Morgan?" she asked in her polished dialect.

"Pretty good, I guess. It's missing something important though. Meat," I giggled.

"Your father told me you were trying to eat healthier. I thought this would be a nice way to start."

I can't even lie. That statement pissed me off.

My father had told this lady I was fat. And this lady was trying to force me to lose weight by eating like this. On top of that, was she trying to offer me a "healthier start" as if my mother had not already?

"Look lady, my mother has already given me the healthy

'start' I need! And just because my body type doesn't meet the standard of *your* beauty, doesn't mean I gotta change myself to ensure that it does!"

"Excuse me?" she responded, shocked. "I was not trying to offend you. Nor would I ever compare myself to your mother. I was just offering you something new."

"We don't need anything or any*one* new around here!" I stormed up and out of my seat.

"Morgan!" my sister tried to calm me down.

"Manuel! I could use your help here. I will not take anymore disrespect."

"She tried to disrespect our mother first!"

Why couldn't this hired helper dismiss herself? I thought.

"Girls, girls. I need you to speak with a lot more respect to Miss Cindy. She certainly isn't going anywhere so you better start treating her more like family," my dad states sternly.

What the hell did that mean? I was confused.

"Family?" Daphne repeated. "I don't think so."

"Like it or not, darling, she's here to stay."

"Oh really?" I asked. "We'll see about that!"

"Yea, seriously dad. We don't need her here. We need our mother!" Even Daphne had turned up a little. The emotions were running real high tonight. My father was at a loss for words.

Tears filled my eyes, just thinking about my father trying to replace mom with this new woman. Life was crumbling into a million pieces. I thought I was over it. The pain of my mother's loss was supposed to have passed. I should have been stronger and wiser. Instead I was weakened and felt like I was losing more and more control.

I couldn't enjoy my family. I couldn't enjoy my meals. I couldn't enjoy my friendships. I couldn't enjoy my extracurricular activities. I could no longer enjoy the one guy who had shown me a little love and respect. I couldn't even enjoy a moment in time just being me. The life of a teenager simply *sucked*.

Dear Diary, Tuesday September 25th

I needed to let my recent troubles off my chest. And there were not many people I could trust.

During cheerleading practice, I called out to Patricia.

"Girl, you are killing it out here!" I paid her a compliment.

"You think so?" she blushed. "I hope the captains see me."

We sat down on one of the benches for a break.

"Trust me, you're hard to miss. And who would've thought the tables would've turned this way?"

"Word," she agreed. "The struggle was real for me this time last year. How are you holding up with all the changes?"

I was glad she asked. "Pat, I seriously don't know where to begin! I feel completely out of my element in every single way. Whether I'm at home or at school, I can't get comfortable. I'm missing my mom and I'm missing my friends. I don't know how much more I can take."

Negative emotions were filling me up inside again. I cold not escape them.

"Well, your friends ain't going anywhere, girl. We're here for you- always. And your mom is still living in your heart. You have to make her proud. That's the only way you'll find peace. Live for her. Smile for her. Talk to her."

"You always got something good to say, girl!" Patricia's words truly did speak some life into me. "But you guys are all on a different path now. Y'all got the squad moving. Tiffany over there pregnant as a mofo. Even my dude Troy made the football team and I'm feeling left behind."

"Life happens," she continued. "Don't sweat it. Everyone has to adjust to their personal life decisions. But everything we experience is gonna produce growth. Right now, you may not need to be cheering your heart out while you're still mourning. You need to heal. Find a way to do that while fulfilling your greatest passions. That's what I had to do last year- I joined the poetry club and got a chance to speak my honest mind at *the Cave* one night. It was so freeing."

"I feel you girl. There actually is something I've been meaning to pitch to the squad leaders. I've been hesitant because I don't think I can do it alone but let me sleep on it some more. I'm sure I'll come up with a plan that will solve my problems and a few others."

"That's what I'm talking about! You got the juice girl.. All you gotta do is pour it out!"

"You certainly are the poet, Pat! Thanks," I smiled.

"No problem, hon'. I'm getting back to practice though. If you're around by the end, let's chat some more."

"I think I'm gonna head out now, actually. There's some family business I need to handle."

"Sounds good. Later girl," Patricia picked up her pom poms and headed back to practice.

I hurried myself home to make good with my dad.

Dear Diary, Thursday September 27th

Patricia was absolutely right. Maybe it was fate that I couldn't perform with the squad for a little while. With a brand new family dynamic, I need to spend more time at home with my sister and my dad. Never mind the stranger that was lurking around. It was our house and it was time to make it a home again.

I went straight home from school today. I didn't stop to check out anyone's football practice or cheer rehearsal. My sister had a tennis match today and I was determined to be there for her.

I knew my dad was taking her to this one and I was hoping to catch the ride.

When I arrived home, I saw that his car was parked in the driveway. *Yes! I made it.*

Inside the house, my sister was scurrying around to collect her things, finally making her way to the door. My dad was searching for his keys. And then, I saw Miss Cindy reach for her jacket to come along.

"Wait, where is she going, dad?" I asked, as respectfully as I could.

"Miss Cindy wanted to check out the match. Daphne said it's fine." I glared at Daphne for that one. *How could she so easily let this woman in?* It was bimbos like this that caused mom's insecurity leading to her death.

"Morgan, we can't keep fighting this. Mom's gone. We have to move on."

I couldn't believe my ears. My sister was always a bit insensitive to me and mom. This was why we were never any closer. Her priorities were so selfishly aligned. If it wasn't about her sport, it was about her. Never did she ever stop to think about the way her decisions affected me.

"I hate this family!" I yelled. "All y'all want to do is act like mom never existed when in truth, she's the only one who ever did! She listened to me, spoke to me, related to me, cooked, and even taught me a few lessons."

"I understand how you feel, Morgan. I lost her too," Daphne explained. "Trust me, I feel you. But the pain will not destroy me. I'm trying to heal in my own way. And we don't have to erase any old memories just because we're building new ones."

"Well, I'm not ready for new ones. I want this lady gone. Why does she have to come to our family functions? She doesn't belong!"

"I'm here to support each one of you," Miss Cindy started. "So if you need me to fall back, I'll stay behind. It is okay."

"No way," my dad said. "This is no longer about you, it's about respect. Morgan will have to learn some sooner than later."

Here we go! My dad was turning on me again.

"I thought this woman was here for the *money*, dad. Why does she get the *power*, too? Is she another one of your conquests?" I asked, truly crossing all boundaries and knowing I'd be in for it.

"Morgan!" he yelled at me. "Stop it at once! Another word and we're heading out without you."

I had to quit then. I did not want to miss Daphne's meet, especially if it meant my dad would be attending it with the housekeeper alone.

Daphne jumped in however, in my defense.

"Wait, but dad. She's right. Is this hired help or is she more to you? Because the way you got her clinging to us is making things look a lot more personal than professional."

My dad and Miss Cindy looked at each other with guilt. I knew there was more to the story.

My father takes a seat. "Truth is, girls, Cindy and I have known each other for quite some time now. She and I never had a relationship though, until we were introduced professionally for the purpose of this job. Since then, I have begun to fall for her. And I hope you can grow to love her too."

"Oh, hell to the nah!" Daphne screamed out. "That's scandalous daddy and you know it! How are we supposed to believe you weren't cheating on mommy with her?"

"I told you the whole truth, girls. And that's all there is to it."

"Look," Miss Cindy said standing around scared and confused. "I'm going to head out. I'll catch an Uber because this is just too much for me right now. And you need to work this out with your daughters."

Finally, the lady recognized it was time to leave. She flew quickly out the door.

"Look what you did," my father said, slouching into his chair with defeat. "I need you girls to understand the major loss I encountered as well. Your mother was more than just my wife. She was my best friend, my confidant, my heart, my mind and my soul. We had issues with intimacy but that would and could never change the fact that I loved her and miss her every second of every day. She brought me joy, peace, love, patience, comfort, and so much more. I need someone to fill that void. A man cannot live with that emptiness every day of his life."

"Well, guess what, dad? A teenager can't either but guess what... here we are in emptiness- living it!" I exclaimed.

"We seriously need to leave guys," Daphne said. "But I can tell you both- we are all facing the same heartbreak. And we need to stop fighting each other on how we handle it. Each of our healing processes is gonna be different. And no one can get mad at it anymore."

I was still stunned at what we'd learned and experienced just now. Daphne was a lot stronger than me to verbalize such a candid perspective.

With the air cleared out and the room a little less crowded, my emotions were at ease. I took a deep breathe and offered everyone an apology.

"Daphne's right. And I'm sorry, dad. I love you both but I'm hurting seemingly more than you guys are."

"There's no way that's true," he said. "We are all hurting in our own way. We just need to talk it out so we're all clear when support is needed."

"I agree," Daphne said. "Now, can we go?"

"Yes ma'am!" my dad jumped up and out of his rout, ready to embark on a positively victorious day for my sister.

My sister did not play her best game today resulting in one of very few losses for her, but we had a major win as a family.

There was certainly more to figure out with this Miss Cindy character but I promised my sister I would be a little more understanding to dad's needs next time.

"Fine!" was all I could say. I hope when I express my needs someday, he will be just as understanding.

VOLUME 18: ME VS. YOU

Dear Diary,   *Friday October 5th*

I had no choice but to sit in on the bench during today's home game. The cheerleaders did their thing on the dance floor. I was especially impressed by my girls Tammy and Patricia who took front center spots in the formation.

The captains wanted me to learn the routines and witness it all in action. They made it seem as though it was to be an educational experience for me. But I knew the truth, they wanted to torture me for being fat. It was a huge slap in the face knowing the message they truly intended. *Look at all the skinny girls on the floor. You couldn't possibly fit into the lineup looking the way you do.*

For once, I wasn't phased. I was working out and working on something that was gonna blow everyone's minds!

After the game, as the cheer team and the ball players gathered around trying to decide where we were going to celebrate tonight's victory, Jay approached me.

"Look at you slimming down for your boy!" he said. If anything else had come out of his mouth, the sound of his voice would have disgusted me. But to hear someone actually take notice to my weight loss efforts, I couldn't help but crack a smile.

"You don't want none of this, Jay. Leave me alone," I teased.

"You know I can't resist you," he continued.

"That's not what you told me on the island," I reminded him of his final words to me during our summer vacation.

"Your boy grew up a little. I'm sorry about that, queen."
He was really trying to say all the right things tonight.

"Sounds good," I said. "But I gotta catch up with my girls."

"We're heading over to the Cave. I hope to catch you at the spot."

"We'll see."

Of course the squad was pulling to wherever the players were going to be. So naturally, we ended up at the Cave.

There were several tables reserved for the teams and a live band playing on the stage tonight.

My friends and I ordered a pie of pizza and fruit tea to go along with it. It was a specialty drink they offered here that was made of fresh fruits and assorted tea flavors.

The music was on point and the vibes were all the way right. I even felt up to dancing on the dance floor. Usually, I would never put myself on display amongst the skinny folks. But tonight, Jay's comment had me feeling myself.

He must have noticed me getting my groove on because he stepped right up to me and began moving with my body.

He put his hands up on my hips and when I dipped, he dipped, we dipped!

I couldn't front either, it brought me back to some of the moments we shared earlier this summer. Jay had some power moves and I couldn't deny it.

So when he invited me to walk home with him after this celebration, it was easy for me to give in. We had already been having so much fun. Why stop now?

At the back of my mind, I thought about Troy who no longer had time for me. I wished it was him getting down with me tonight. But Troy was focused now and on everything but me. At this point, it's you vs. me and he made it clear where his priorities were going forward. I was doing him a favor by moving on, even if that meant moving backward and messing with Jay.

It should have made me think twice when I was leaving and caught a glimpse of Troy's twin brother throw the deuces up at Jay. But I was set on being adored and appreciated by someone tonight. It was a feeling I couldn't turn away.

I had never been to a guy's house before so this was both chill and quite a thrill.

When I stepped into his house, a gentle aroma filled the air, much like it did Jay's hotel room at the resort. It instantly brought on feeling of comfort. He took my belongings and placed it into a closet by the front door. He was neat and organized. He led me into a den area with a flat screen television and surround sound speakers affixed throughout the room. There were musical instruments on display and awards hanging around the walls.

"Is someone in your family a musician?" I asked.

"Yea my dad is, how'd you know?" he smiled with sarcasm.

"Just a lucky guess," I joked back.

"Yea he's a producer. He works mostly with Caribbean artists but I've seen him do it all. He hates that I chose sports over the arts but hey, I gotta be me."

"True," I agreed. "And your great at it so keep up the good work."

"Oh yea?" he neared me with his lips. "What else am I good at?"

"You already know," I teased.

"Tell me."

"You tell me what you like about *me* first..." I wondered if there was anything at all that he admired about me. I knew sex was the aim here and now but was there anything more?

He began a trail of kisses from my lips down to my neck. "These lips, this neck, your chest..."

I guess it was all totally physical for him. He saw nothing more in me. He didn't notice how genuine I was in taking interest in him, in admiring his talents, sharing his passion for sports & fitness, our musical appreciation, nor my comfort. It was sickening how much greatness guys missed in the midst of their selfishness.

I still wanted and needed the physical fulfillment he was set out to bring me. I appreciated the touches on my skin and the taste of his lips on mine. His moves made me feel like I was living for a moment and not just existing in my pain.

However, I knew whatever I experienced tonight would be out of my reach by tomorrow. Jay would act like we didn't share this moment of bliss. He'll pretend like he doesn't know me all that well. He may nod his head at me in school but I wouldn't get a hug or even a few words of acknowledgement.

By now, Jay had moved his mouth to every area of my body. It was alluring. My body shook with pleasure. I tried to ignore my thoughts and live in the moment just as he was.

It was a wonder to me how guys could move completely out of their minds and wholly within their bodies. At this very moment, I couldn't separate my clouded thoughts from these tender feelings. As much as I wanted to fulfill a physical need, I had an even greater emotional one.

I needed love and appreciation. I needed support and peace of mind. I needed my dignity.

Ultimately, I was enjoying the contact between Jay and I

but I was turned off by the disvalue he displayed for me as a person. *Would he dismiss me tonight the way he did at the resort and the pool party? Would he tell me that this awesome night meant nothing more than a few moments of pleasure? Would he remind me that I'm not worth anything to him again?*

My heart could not take the disappointment. My body couldn't take the empty indulgence. My soul couldn't be tampered with again.

I had to leave.

I pushed him off of me just before he prepared to enter my entire being.

"What's up, girl?" he was confused.

"Absolutely nothing," I said putting the clothes he ripped off, back on.

"What you mean? Ain't you enjoying this?" he asked.

"Not enough," I replied. There was no way he'd understand much more than that.

"So hold up, you're gonna leave me like this?" he stood up naked and aroused, hoping I would jump back onboard.

As tempting as it was, I needed much more than that to satisfy me tonight. I chose my to consider my desires over his.

"Believe me, I'm at a huge loss tonight too," I walked out, grabbed my things from the front closet and ran home.

VOLUME 19: MORE TO ME

Dear Diary,   *Wednesday October 10ᵗʰ*

When I returned to school after the weekend, there was hell to pay for leaving Jay high and dry.

I was getting all kinds of funny looks from the basketball team. One of them even called me, "blue baller!" as I passed their table in the cafeteria. *Whatever that meant…*

I wasn't phased by any of it, though. Jay had his chance to use me one too many times.

I know I was wrong for agreeing to go to his house, but I was expecting something more from him that last time. Something different.

But for some reason, he had never looked at me deep enough. He was so focused on his own needs, he had not even an inkling about any of mine. It wasn't fair.

After the friendship I had shared with Troy, I could sense the difference between a dude who saw me for me versus one who only saw his own selfish gains. There was a new encounter with pleasure that Troy introduced me to. It truly made me feel like a person of value.

When I hated myself for being big and fat and rejected, he made me feel beautiful and fine and accepted. I needed more of that.

However, when I went to stop by Troy's football practice today, he turned away as I approached.

Oh boy, I thought. *He must have heard about my encounter with Jay. Whether he knew how I walked out on him or not, it had to hurt.*

This time, I had done too much. I knew it would get back to

him that I left the Cave with Jay. I don't know why I let the loneliness and insecurity get the best of me that night.

I continuously allowed the feelings I had for myself eat away at me. I let it corrode my decision making. And this time, I had hurt the one person who deserved my love.

"Troy!" I called out.

He continued to ignore me and remained focused on his drills.

I ran all the way up to him on the field, refusing to give up.

He looked at me coldly, "this isn't the time or place for this, Morgan. Please go."

"Well damn," I stood there stunned. I had never seen him so serious.

I had no choice but to walk away.

Once again, I messed up. Somehow, someway, I had to win Troy back. And next time, I'm playing for keeps.

Dear Diary,   *Thursday October 18th*

I wasn't able to concentrate on homework today. I couldn't get over my guilt nor my loneliness.

I went online and searched: *How to Get a Man Back*

The internet always delivered.

DiaryDiscussions.com read:

There are 3 main rules to every game. When it comes to getting your man back, keep it that simple:

1) Apologize
2) Tell him what you miss about him
3) Show him how much you care (letter, speech, gift, song)

Disclaimer: *We're assuming you're trying to get him back because you did him wrong. So make it right.* *xoxo* *DD*

I loved this site for its simplicity. I could do all of the above.

And so I did.

I was even able to post the poem I wrote on the site, anonymously at that!

CurvyCat posts on Thursday October 18 at 4:38pm:

<u>Baby Love</u>

This feeling here's an infant, totally brand new
But it's time to grow up and say how much I'm missing you
I miss you in the morning and in the afternoon
I miss you in the evening and underneath the moon
It's like I can't escape you, you're crowding up my head
I need you in my life like butter needs its bread
You're the one that showed me love, from the very start
You opened up the door to my broken heart
The kinda friend I need to last always and forever
To hug me up when I feel down, to let go, never
I'm here for you alone, you don't have to be afraid
Mistakes are of the past, this here's a new day
'Cause now I know what love is, from you and from myself
I listened to your heart beat and felt exactly what you felt

Dear Diary,   *Tuesday afternoon October 23ʳᵈ*

I couldn't help but overhear that Troy made a winning pass in last night's game. He was off to a great season!

It was so unfortunate that we weren't on speaking terms though. I wanted so badly to show him some love. He deserved lunch, on me. But I was lucky enough to get a hello from him in the hallways.

Walking past the exercise room, I could smell him. Walking in, I feel his presence.

I had to show him how sorry I was. He needed to know there was more to me than jealous insecurity. He needed to see my growth. I had to show him my adoration.

I waited for football practice to end after school today. This was the perfect time to share my poem with him. It was the only way back into his heart.

Dear Diary,   *Wednesday October 24ᵗʰ*

My plan had worked. Troy finally took the time to hear me out. I mean, I didn't give him much of a choice this time. I damn near followed him from the field to his locker room and waited for him to get dressed.

"What do you want from me, Morgan?" he said while rushing out.

"You, Troy. Your friendship at least. An *us* at the very most."

"Aren't you good on guys at this point?"

"Nope, I've been at my worst without you. And I want to say sorry. I haven't been honest with you about my feelings."

"What feelings?" he stopped to give me his attention.

"I really like you, Troy. Always have. And I've wanted more than just a friendship with you."

"Doesn't seem so. From what I've heard you're good."

"Listen to what *I'm* saying now, Troy," and I pulled out the poem.

That was all he needed to see. He grabbed me up and gave me our first kiss. It was bliss. ☺

Dear Diary,   Friday October 26th

I went to cheerleading practice today, as there was a huge pep talk scheduled.

The captains were extremely proud of the team. We had won yet another game and of course the cheerleaders take a portion of the credit for that.

Then they announced that we received a grant check. The cheer team was awarded $10,000 to make a difference in our school's community.

It was the missing piece to my puzzle. My idea would fit perfectly. I finally found my purpose for staying on the squad. Now I had to make sure the captains knew it too.

VOLUME 20: MUSIC MADNESS

Dear Diary,   *Monday October 30th*

My mother had shared something important with me before she left us. She told me that if those cheerleaders didn't want me, I should create a squad of my own. One that isn't superficial, one that uplifts and inspires, one that prides themselves of helping others.

So I asked the captains if I could meet with them and propose my great idea. It would fit right in line with the cheerleader's grant award and my personal goals.

I wanted to kickoff a training program to get or keep students in shape.

"Once or twice a week, we could get a personal trainer for students who need fitness tips. We can take them to the exercise room and show them how I lost the weight. We'd do exercises, dance routines, and workouts motivated by music. And I even know a guy who wants to help..." I went on to explain how I intended to fight to keep my position on the squad. I shared this concept of Cheerleaders being "Care Leaders" and extending an arm out to the greater school community in a way that promotes health, beauty, and fitness. There was no way we could lose.

I even enlisted my friends into this whole ordeal and they agreed to help if ever I needed them.

"Okay," one of the captains said. "Make it happen, Morgan."

"And don't forget your next weigh-in is coming up next week."

I had forgotten about that. But with my new responsibility to run the Music Madness project I proposed, maybe I could kill two birds with one stone.

Dear Diary,   *Friday November 3rd*

With my weigh just days away, this was my final opportunity to get myself in shape.

I was spending all my lunch breaks in the fitness center, and much of my practice time as well. I needed to prove I could do this so I could rejoin the performance team as well as lead the Music Madness initiative.

And so I created my own 30 minute workout routine and followed through with it every chance I got. It consisted of cardiovascular exercises on the treadmill and elliptical, a light jog, weight machines that strengthened the back and core, the upper and lower leg, and the arms. Then, a five minute stretch followed, and an aerobic dance routine concludes.

I was on a roll once I got used to this workout regime. It was empowering and made me feel alive. The sweat dripping off my body displayed my efforts. The sore muscles confirmed I had put in that work.

This part of the project was madness. I couldn't wait until I could add the music!

Dear Diary,   *Monday November 6th*

I spent my weekend staying far away from both family and the foreigner. Daphne and Miss Cindy were getting undeniably close and I wanted nothing to do with it.

I focused on making cool posters to promote the Care Leaders Music Madness project. I created a playlist of songs that I wanted to showcase on the kickoff date. I exercised, I danced, and I practiced my introductory speech all day and all night.

I was ready.

Dear Diary,

Tuesday November 7th

My weigh in was today! I was nervous the entire day, especially when I got to the fitness center and realized the scale was broken. *Ugh!*

I was hoping to check and see where I stand. I needed to know my status before the captains found out.

So during my lunch period, I made my way to the nurse's office. I needed to surpass the line of students needing care and get to the scale. But the line was too long. The nurse was too busy. The scale was already occupied.

So I head over to the physical education department to utilize theirs.

Thankfully, their electronic scale was available. Once I stepped on, I squeezed my eyes shut scared to find out what it would reveal.

I was pleased to see I had successfully lost not just the 10 pounds I was supposed to, but in fact, 11 pounds! Thank goodness! I was elated.

But wouldn't you know, when I got to cheer practice today, excited for the captains' weigh in, their old fashioned analog scale weighed me in at only a 9 pound weight loss.

"There must be a mistake!" I exclaimed. "I weighed myself earlier and the results were greater."

"Well, did you happen to eat lunch sometime after?"

"Maybe," I replied. "Are you really gonna hold that against me though?"

"No, I guess not. You can perform with us again as long as the uniform fits you without even a hint of a bulge..."

"I don't see how she's going to have time to learn all of this season's routines while she's executing the grant project though. That's a pretty huge priority."

I was so happy with what I was hearing. I went from having no purpose on the team to having two. I would make certain I fit into my uniform without a problem. And as for the project, I'm gonna kill that too!

"Look ladies, I got this!" I affirmed to the captains. "And I won't let you down!"

Dear Diary, *Wednesday November 22nd*

In just over two weeks, We kicked off the Music Madness program with a school wide pep rally today. It was surreally a success.

I couldn't believe the support and teamwork I received fro my friends. My boo Troy got the whole football team involved. They were the male counterparts we needed to get the guys pumped about the initiative. And pumped they were!

We used a portion of the grant funds to host a photo shoot with the cheer squad prior. With these images, we created public service announcement posters and posted them throughout the gymnasium.

"Every *body* can dream. Beauty is in every *body*. Move to improve. Music is the mood of the moment. Make your body match your mind." These slogans were amongst the many we had displayed around the room.

During the pep rally, all students got a chance to take part in various photo shoots throughout the event. We hired a DJ to play ongoing music from my fitness playlist. We had the *Juice Vibes* vendor there to whip up smoothies for everyone.

The energy in the room was everything I imagined it to be.

Music blasting, people moving, cheerleaders chanting. The madness had begun.

Then, we announced a series of fitness sessions that the Care Leaders would be hosting. The footballers would be facilitating the weight room sessions. The cheerleaders led aerobic exercises. We hired a personal trainer and nutritionist to assist attendees with personal goals.

The captains even looked at me during the event and smiled. Jana gave me a thumbs up. This project was a huge success and we were just getting started.

Dear Diary,   *Friday November 25th*

This Thanksgiving, my dad had invited his parents, our grandparents, over. It was a sad holiday for us all. It was the first time we broke bread for thanksgiving dinner and my mother wasn't there to join us.

To make matters worse, Miss Cindy was.

The day was quiet as my paternal grandmother gathered some old photos of us all and displayed them in the den. My granddad had old family films to share. My sister, grandmother, and I cleared out the last items from my mother's closet. She had some awesome stuff.

We played a few games before dinner. Then at dinner, my dad dropped the biggest bomb.

He shares with our table of six that he and Miss Cindy are indeed involved. *Ugh!* I thought. Was this going to be the topic of the table?

"We actually met because of your mother," he addressed Daphne. "She wanted us get additional help around the house as she was planning to start part time work."

Lies! I thought. He could say just about anything now that mom was gone.

He looked at me and said, "She especially thought you'd like her meal prep."

"Oh, really?" I questioned with a bit of sarcasm.

"Yes," Miss Cindy replied. "She and I met at the church. We did many soup kitchens together. She always talked about you, Morgan, wanting us to meet. I work so much though, I couldn't attend as often as she did."

This was brand new information. The pieces of her stories with my mom did seem to fit though. All I could wonder is, *How could she find it appropriate to be dating a friend's widower?*

"Since our tragedy, it's like Cindy has brought the love of God into my heart. I have only found peace with my wife's passing because of her."

Those were some strong words, Daddy. I thought, *you're getting way too attached to the help.*

"I took this family on as a client but can see myself quitting just to be family."

"Wow," was the general response around the table.

As I looked puzzled and Daphne looked proud, my dad continued. "With that said, we are pleased to announce that we are expecting a little love child together!"

I was stunned and irate. My dad had just crushed my already fragile heart. *How could he be keeping this bimbo around? And to make a child? Would that make her a part of our family for real? That was absurd!*

I was eating a most delicious Cajun turkey with sweet potatoes and gravy but I lost my entire appetite at once.

As everyone relished in their joy, I ravished in my disgust. I went up to my room and sulked the rest of the evening.

My grandmother eventually came to speak to me but I was so broken inside, I didn't hear a word she said.

VOLUME 21: MAKE ME WHOLE

Dear Diary,   *Sunday December 4th*

I hadn't spoken to my dad in days. I grew more and more hateful of him by the day. Where could I find the space in my heart to love him again?

I opted to attend church this weekend.

The sermon was all about love languages.

"God has given us all the most fruitful of his gifts. Love," the guest pastor spoke with such passion. I did not want to miss a word. "Love gives us the power to do good. It gives us the power to see good. It is the very making of God himself."

That was an interesting concept. Love was powerful. I just never saw it as a power. Until now.

"'What is love?' people often wonder. 'How does it feel? How do you know it's real? 1 Corinthians 13:4-8 says it all:

Love is patient, love is kind. It does not envy, it does not boast, it is not proud. It does not dishonor others, it is not self seeking, it is not easily angered, it keeps no record of wrongs. Love does not delight in evil but rejoices with the truth. It always protects, always trusts, always hopes, always perseveres."

That really was clear. Love was unlike any experience I'd ever had. Only with Troy in mind, I could envision true love flourishing. But only time would tell.

"There is a book by an old friend of mine, Gary Chapman. Met him at a teaching seminar. It's called, 'The Five Love Languages'. He writes about the ways we express our love to each other. We all have a different way, you see. Conflict, hurt, pain and even hate only come about because we don't understand each other's languages."

Languages of love? I had never heard of it. But I wanted to know more.

"There are 5 ways that we, in the human form, display God's love amongst ourselves. The fun part is figuring out which one is your way. And then your partners, your child, your biggest hater even." We all laughed. "Hey, haters need love too. They need it the most because they're lacking the most."

He wasn't lying about that!

"So listen, there's quality time, words of affirmation, gifts, acts of service, and physical touch. Quality time is about spending time with a person, the way most of us spend money. Daily, carefully, and thoughtfully." *Maybe that was my language. I loved hanging out with my friends, my family when I actually had a solid one, and even my new boo.*

"Words of affirmation is about using the power of the tongue, and even written word, to tell someone exactly how you feel. No shade, as the young people say." *I enjoyed hearing nice things from others but it was rare that it ever happened.*

"Gifts are not always material. It is the act of giving of yourself tangibly. It shows that you are thought of even when you're not in each other's presence." *Gifts are nice too,* I thought, *but I wouldn't want anyone knowing my sizes.*

"Acts of service is doing for one another without the expectation of getting anything back. Just doing something nice to bring a smile to a loved ones face." That was often what Troy did for me. He was careful and helpful to me, never expecting anything in return- except a smile.

"And physical touch, is more than sexual. It includes affection, intimacy, closeness, attachment, connection, and communication. It sends a message of comfort. A simple handshake can bring about a connection. A hug can offer peace. A hug and a kiss is acknowledgement of another's being." *Now that was one I hadn't experienced. That was what I needed.*

"Oh, I know which one most of you are thinking. But it goes deeper than that. And like I said, its fun to figure out your language. But the challenge is knowing another's and speaking to them in a way they understand. That is true love. And that's the way God expects us to live. By giving and receiving love. In any language."

"Can we all promise to live in love? Can we all live in God's peace? Can we spread his gifts throughout his universe? The life he has given us through waters, and plants, and our natural existence- all made with love. Can we rejoice at his wonders? Can we appreciate the abundance of his love? Can we seek to experience his joy?"

I thought about this. *Could I?* It was a challenge for me lately. I was suffering so bad. Love was absent in my home.

"Think about the greatest pain you have felt. With love, it is erased. With the gift of peace, it is gone. Longsuffering is no more! Live with love for God. Love for self. Love for others. There is a verse I think you need to hear. When you are down and out, can't forgive, can't even smile, only his word makes it plain:

1 Corinthians 13:13 And now these three remain: faith, hope, and love; but the greatest of these is love.

Faith is trusting and believing in what you know God can do. Hope is optimism, positivity, and confidence that the best is yet to come. Love is the relationship you build when you give your best. You can build it within yourself. You can build it with a partner or loved one. You can mold the pieces of a broken heart together, broken friendships, absentee family members. Pursue love to live in love. Acknowledge the love of others. Speak the languages of love."

The speaker gave me every bit of the word I needed. It was time for me to build this love thing. I needed to make me whole again. I would have to pursue love within my home or I may live with hate in my heart forever.

Here we go...

As I was heading out of the church building, ready to embark on a long walk home, someone called my name.

She had an accent. An all too familiar one. It was my housekeeper. My father's lady. The mother of his child. *What could she possibly have to say to me?*

"Morgan, you look beautiful!"

Those were words I had never heard. It felt really good.

"Thanks," I couldn't help but crack a smile.

"I recognize that dress from your mom's collection. It fits you so well. You could honestly model that." Miss Cindy continued, gently touching the fabric of my mother's satin dress.

"Yea, I was surprised I fit into her old clothes," I was instantly drawn to the conversation about my mom.

"She and I would pray for hours on end after services and some days we would shop, get coffee, and even talk. She was a wise woman. I learned a lot from her. And I'm sure you did too."

"Yea, I sure did. And I'm still learning from her. Believe me." I contemplated on memories of my mother.

"I know. Same here." Miss Cindy looked off into a distance. The anguish she expressed seemed as genuine as mine. It was the first time I had expressed empathy for her. All along, I only felt she owed me hers.

I offered her my gentle words, "I learned to keep love close. So my mom lives here in my heart. If you miss her that much, you can keep a piece of her in yours too."

"You're absolutely right," she smiled at me. "Would you like a ride home?"

I couldn't believe I was giving in and giving this woman a chance. But she had opened up to me in just a matter of seconds. We connected through touch, words, and time in just moments. Then, here she was offering me an act of service. She was showing me the love of God. I couldn't refuse it any longer.

"Sure," I agreed. "Can we stop for ice cream or something though? My treat." It was all I could offer as a gift of my love.

"I know an amazing frozen yogurt spot you would like. Your mother actually introduced it to me. How does that sound?"

"Sounds like an even better idea!" I was excited for this woman to take me down the memory lane she shared with my mom.

In an instant, I decided to let go of the hate and pain I was holding onto. I had to let love in one way or another. I could no longer judge her for her actions and decisions. All I could do was live with love and find my own peace. God, karma, and luck would take care of the rest.

VOLUME 22: FIRST THINGS FIRST

Dear Diary,   *Friday December 9ᵗʰ*

I needed some quality time with Troy after all I had been dealing with at home.

I knew Miss Cindy wouldn't be working the weekend and was probably travelling with my dad. Daphne would be sleeping in early to prepare for her practice tomorrow morning.

So I offered to meet Troy out for dinner at a burger spot then head over to my place after.

Problem was, I got there before him and didn't have enough discipline to wait for him. It had been a very long time since I'd stepped foot in a burger joint. Heck, it was ages since I'd been able to eat or even *smell* a burger.

I was aroused the moment I walked inside. The menu of pictures and assortment of sauce flavors drew me in.

I opted to order just one before Troy arrived. I was hoping to sneak one in and finish it before he would even notice.

But Troy was running late and I was extremely hungry.

With every minute I sat there idle, I questioned whether or not Troy was coming at all. And so I ordered another.

My heart grew heavy with confusion. Maybe Troy no longer wanted me. He was probably relishing in the glory of being a star athlete. There was probably some cuter, thinner chick giving him all the attention a teenage boy needed. *What could he possibly want with me anymore?*

I ordered another sandwich with fries on the side. This time, I even got a milkshake, hoping it would ease the concern in my mind. Every burger I ordered came with a different sauce and additional toppings. I was in food heaven but knew there would be hell to pay.

I was stepping back into old habits, overeating, and not checking the calories I was consuming. There was no one there to stop me. No one who cared.

I ate savagely for an entire hour until I noticed Troy outside and across the street.

That's when reality hit. *I was a cow and eating like one too!*

I couldn't face him. He would take one look at me and realize how awful a person I am.

So I ran out of the spot. I saw him waving me down. He caught up to me touched my arm.

"Morgan, I'm so sorry I'm late. Our game ran over. The quarterback got injured. Then I got confused when I saw the burger joint..."

More than the lateness, I was concerned about my meal choices. Even Troy was put off by it. I felt awful inside so I must have looked it too. I couldn't stick around. I had to rid my body of this food before I could face anyone again. I just shook my head and distanced myself from him.

"Wait!" he said. "Morgan, it's okay."

But I was already hurrying off. I was embarrassed by my undisciplined behavior. After taking off the weight I needed to, here I was again. I was letting myself go. No one would love me this way. I couldn't even love myself.

I ran home and took a laxative. Surely that would help me empty my stomach.

However, it only made me feel worse.

My stomach tightened. I heard the rumbling sounds of a

stomach ache starting. I crouched at my knees in my shared bathroom, trying to find a comfortable position for myself. Nothing soothed the cramping pains I was feeling.

I sat by the bathtub and I tried to retain some ice cold tap water. I opened my mouth to drink it all up and ended up hitting my head on the faucet. I sat beside the tub, finally giving up. The physical and emotional pain I felt was too great a burden to bear. I closed my eyes and suffered there in aching silence.

Moments later, I was awakened by my sister.

"Someone's here to see you," she came into the bathroom, half asleep.

""Who?" I said drowsily.

"You know someone named Troy? He's been banging on the front door for too long. I almost called the cops."

"Don't do that," I got up, with Daphne's help.

"I didn't. But seriously, who's dude?"

"That's my boo from school. Where is he, though?"

"Right downstairs. Get yourself together, girl. Go talk to him."

"Okay, okay. Can you just send him up?"

"You sure?" my sister side eyed me. I must have been an even bigger mess now than I was before.

"You're right. Just make him wait."

As I looked into the mirror at my disheveled hair, smeared makeup and displaced jewelry, I realized I needed some more time alone.

And then, my body reacted in agreement. The laxative had finally kicked in.

It was quite a while before I could step before Troy with confidence. He would never understand the actions I had taken tonight. So I never went downstairs to explain them.

Dear Diary,   *Saturday December 10th*

I heard Troy call out my name a few times. The house was eerily silent. His voice echoed through the hallways and up the spiral staircase.

"Come," I conjured up the strength to reply.

I had to stop playing games with Troy. He had given me love and comfort in every way that God had described. Patience, kindness, and keeping no record of wrong. He was all that and more.

I wanted to give it all back. I wanted him to experience my tender love in return.

So this weekend while my dad was away on business, I planned to give it *all* to him.

I heard Troy walking up the stairs. I heard him walk in the wrong direction, try different doors, and soon, he entered my room.

"Baby, how are you?"

"Not good," I replied.

"What happened last night? Why did you leave me?"

"You were so very late, Troy. Disrespectfully late. I was confused and concerned."

"But I showed up," he defended.

"Yea but the damage was already done. I sat in that Burger Hut for an entire hour, stuffing my face away."

"Stuffing your face with burgers?!"

I put my head down, disappointed in myself once again. "I know. Which is why I couldn't face you."

"I don't get it. You think I would judge you. For that?" he asked.

"Yes," I confessed. "Everyone judges me that way. What I eat, what size I am, how I dress... It's always been the focus when people look at me. They don't see me for me- ever. I've been shaping up- literally- ever since I met you. But last night, I lost all control..."

"First things first, Morgan. I would never judge you," he started. "I got nothin' but love for you, especially because you've given me nothin' but love. You have never judged me, you have shown me your truth, and you let me in on your struggle. All of that gives me reasons to cherish you."

He cherished me? That was pretty deep.

"Wow," was all I could say as he leaned over my bedside to embrace me with a hug. "I cherish you too."

That's when I prepared myself to make a bold move. I removed the top layer of my pajama set to expose my lace bra.

I pulled Troy onto the bed and sat on top of him.

"Oh boy," he smiled. "I must have said something you liked."

"Yes you did," I moved my hands all over his soft, squeezable body. "I'm gonna cherish every part of you today."

I buried his face with kisses and sucked on his lips. He shook with pleasure in a way I'd never seen him move before. He put his hands around me and held me tight.

He kissed my neck. I threw my head back as I experienced a most a pleasurable sensation. My hands wandered all over his body. It was the most intimate we had ever been together. It was pure bliss.

Just as I was beginning to remove more clothing, I felt his bulge. I gently reached for it but he took my hand to stop me.

"Morgan, we need to stop and talk."

"Really? Now?" I asked.

"Yea, *right* now."

I put my clothes back on and positioned myself to face him and talk.

"What's up, babe?"

"I'm saving myself," he said.

"From what?" I asked. "For who?"

He laughed a little. "For you, silly. I want to save myself for marriage."

"Really?" I had not known one guy that would actually *choose* to attempt that in this day and age.

"Yes," he continued. "I know it sounds strange but I've been committed to living by the word all my life. So far, I've received so many wonderful blessings for following this path. I don't want to stop now."

"Wow, I certainly wasn't expecting that. Are you sure it's not that I turn you off?" I felt a little shy after my bodily exposure.

"Absolutely not," he rubbed his hands on my back and stomach, then rested them on my leg. "You are the only person that has ever turned me on. But I'm much more pleased by your smile, your touch, and your words of encouragement. The sexual stuff can wait a while. I'm focused on winning games, passing classes, and keeping you smiling."

"I feel you, bruh. But are you seriously waiting 'til marriage? Like seriously, no sex in college? Not even if you're a star athlete?"

"I have goals, girl. I want to be committed to more than temptation and desires of the flesh. We have forever to think about sex. The anticipation will be well worth it in the end, don't you think?"

"Okay, Troy. I hear you." I can't argue with a man with a plan.

"I know you hear it but can you respect it?"

That was a good question. Having already indulged in several sexual experiences, my desires for physical satisfaction were deeper than Troy knew. I craved the physical touch. I desired the closeness of his body against mine.

But for a guy so honest and passionate about his beliefs, I had to be wiling to try. Besides, I wanted to walk that straight path he spoke of. If our love proved strong enough, the wait *will* be well worth it.

"Yes, I definitely respect it."

"Well, what about us. Do you think we can make it to forever?"

That was easy. If Troy and I had gotten through the betrayal, absence, forgiveness, struggle, insecurity, and hardships we'd endured thus far; we had to fight through the rest.

"I think we can make it 'til forever but I doubt the celibacy will make it a month," I answered with all honesty.

"Both will take work," he said.

"I'm down to put in that work," I raised a closed fist and he matched me with his.

"Let's do it," he agreed.

Dear Diary,   *Tuesday December 20th*

We celebrated our annual team holiday party during cheer hours today.

My friends and I were at ease as everyone had finally earned a comfortable spot on the squad. Patricia and I knew the struggle most of all. We had gone from having a spot to losing it and fighting to get back. It was truly the time of year to rejoice.

I was surprised to see Tiffany at the party though. She still had to fulfill the fate of childbirth before ever stepping foot back on the performance floor. She and Tammy were happily assisting with snack distribution, displaying not a care in the world. Tammy's role was always secure.

With donuts and hot chocolate surrounding us, festive décor, cute ugly sweaters on, and holiday music blasting, we could feel every bit of the holiday spirit.

One of the captains interrupted the festivities to make a

special announcement. All eyes turned toward her.

"We are so pleased with this year's team. We have an undefeated basketball and football team thus far and despite the quarterback's latest injury, school pride is at an all time high."

The next senior captain continued, "We have inspired the entire student body to become healthier because of our 'Care Leader' grant. It has brought more support to our club from administrators, parents, and fellow students."

It was cool to hear the Care Leaders program acknowledged. I pondered whether I would receive any credit for that...

"With all that said, we want to award a dedicated leader, organizer, and team player with the Winter Merit Award this season. With her perseverance this year to fulfill the expectations of the previous leadership, through vigorous weight loss and exercise, and for taking the initiative to kick off our Music Madness event, we acknowledge her hard work and commitment."

The statements were becoming more and more familiar to me. Their words were hitting close to home.

"We have seen her fight through adversity, undergo the loss of her dear mother, collaborate with team members within and outside our squad, and organize a highly successful grant funded program, something no cheerleader has ever done before. Congratulations, Morgan Sawyer. On this day, Tuesday December 20th, we honor you with the Winter Merit award and hope you would accept the role of Junior captain going forward."

I stopped in my tracks and put down the frosted donut I was about to stuff into my mouth.

"Me?!" I exclaimed.

"Yes, you, girl!" Patricia said excitedly.

"Go claim your prize!" Tammy urged me out of my seat and up to the platform where the captains were standing.

"O-M-G! Thank you all," I was beyond shocked. "This is totally unexpected."

"And well deserved," Patricia added.

The girls came up to surround me with their hugs. They showed me so much love, I hardly knew how to receive it. Never before had I felt so enamored with pride.

This was true joy. And I sucked it all in.

VOLUME 23: FEELING MYSELF

Dear Diary,   *Friday December 23rd*

Today was the last day of school before the holiday break. Troy came to meet me at cheer practice following his own practice today. He greeted me with a huge smile. He must have news as great as I had received earlier this week.

"Babe, you wouldn't believe this!" He grabbed me up with glee.

"What's up, Troy?" I asked, trying to match his excitement.

"Remember how I told you there was an injury?" I nodded wondering how that could produce any joy. "They offered me the quarterback's position!"

"Oh wow, babe that's awesome!" Congrats! Are you gonna take it?"

"You bet I am! That was always the goal anyhow."

I was truly impressed by the way Troy had leveled up his entire life in less than a year. Everything he told me he wanted, he had been receiving.

"You are truly blessed," I said.

"I know it every time I look at you!" he said. I blushed hard.

"Well damn, you got me feeling myself these days."

"I've always been feeling you," he replied with a juicy kiss to my lips. "'Bout time you realized how it feels."

I couldn't front, it felt good. Not just the love I was receiving, but the joy of working hard at something and succeeding at it too.

Troy knew the exact feeling. He had helped me accomplish so much this year. We had truly teamed up to become an unbreakable force. His admiration for me was unmatched. His forgiveness of me was commendable. I am so glad I gave him a chance at friendship, at partnership, and at love. Moreover, I'm glad he's taken a chance with me.

Dear Diary,   *Sunday December 25th*

Merry Christmas!

This season, I was in great place with my friends. I was in a loving relationship. I was satisfied with the project I created at school. And my body was at it best- or at least I felt it was. But my family needed serious repair.

I needed them all to attend church with me this Christmas. It was finally time to forgive.

With an open heart to accept my dad's decision about Miss Cindy, I invited them all to the service with me.

"Really? Even I have to go?" Daphne resisted.

"It's just one day. Do for me as a gift," I pleaded.

"Okay, that works," she laughed. "I didn't get you anything too hot this year so now we're straight."

I shook my head, "whatever."

Everyone put on their Sunday best this morning. My dad showed his gentlemen quality as he held Miss Cindy's coat, while she placed her arms inside. Daphne who didn't wear dresses often, had on a fitted sweater dress that illuminated her gorgeous body like she didn't even know. I found another designer outfit from my mother's things. *Who knew Calvin Klein made curvy clothing that would fit me so right?*

At the church, we learned about peace. That was really all I needed in my life. Peace of mind and peace within my heart. I needed to make peace with my mother's passing. I couldn't go another year with such a heavy heart. None of us could.

"I know this year has been troubling for many of you. I have had my share of struggle as well. But there is a place of peace waiting for you. Seek it and you will find it."

I hoped he would be more specific. *Where do we find it?* I certainly couldn't control the emptiness I felt from time to time. How could I erase my thoughts and feelings? How would I rebuild trust in my dad, a connection with my sister, and comfort with this new family structure?

"Look to 2 Corinthians 13:11," the speaker continued. "Finally, brothers and sisters, rejoice! Become complete. Be of good comfort, be of one mind, live in peace; and the God of love and peace will be with you."

How? I thought.

"You can only do this with an open mind and an open heart. Look to your brethren for comfort. Look to them for peace. Look to your family for understanding. Live with love. You do not need to search far. It is already there waiting for you to acknowledge it."

My sister turned to me then took my hand. My father took her hand. Miss Cindy smiled at me.

I took a deep breathe, acknowledging the air of peace that was surrounding me in that moment.

Maybe I needed to relax a little. It was time for me to enjoy the presence of those family members that were here. I needed to listen to them, spend more time, and provide them with much needed acts of service. I had to express my love in ways they would understand. They would never leave my side. I never wanted to leave theirs.

After the service, we went out for dinner. It was the first time we had all been out together and in peace.

As we sat in harmony, I felt my mother's presence amongst us. I felt uplifted rather than slighted being at this restaurant she once loved.

I couldn't help but recite a long winded prayer that would unite our entire family once and for all.

Praying for Peace

I pray for peace, I pray for love
I pray for this family and my mother above
I hope for light to see you clear
I need you all, I need you near
I want to cherish you every single chance
I look forward to our father daughter dance
I long to forgive, I long to forget
I want to live life with no more regrets
I want to see this lifetime through
Without the pain or any hate for you
I cry out for my sister D
Whatever happened to you and me?
Our bond's been broken, ripped apart
Though we share one mind, one soul, one heart
We need to love, we need repair
We need each other, who's been doing your hair?
And now we have this unborn child
Who will need us most, he will need our smile
We must unite, share one heartbeat
Let's come together, don't accept defeat
When life is lost, it still goes on
If not in flesh, in spiritual form
Inside our minds, inside our homes
Love lives forever, it's never gone
Bless me up, love me down
I look to you for peace all around

"Amen," everyone said in unison.

The four of us enjoyed a most peaceful meal this evening. No drama and fussing took place. I finally felt whole and not hurt.

My sister and I laughed together again. We made plans to go swimming at Push Fitness during the break.

"Oo!" Miss Cindy exclaimed interrupting all side conversations. She was holding her stomach with gentle discomfort.

"That must be the baby's first kick," my dad smiled.

Daphne and I went over to touch her belly. We each made a miraculous connection with her. It had finally set in, we were having a baby brother.

I had let go of all ill feelings. I was feeling fine. I felt the love. And I felt loved.

Dear Diary, *Wednesday December 28th*

This was the morning Daphne and I were headed out for a swim. It was a true luxury to be able to swim indoors during the wintertime.

As I dressed, I no longer needed to try on an assortment of outfits until I found something I felt comfortable in.

I felt good on the inside and the outside just knowing how much progress had been made in my life.

I had lost over 15 pounds this year, just by eating right and having fun moving my body. I never did get that weight loss surgery I wanted but my mother did, and tragically so, she let me know that I didn't need it. My friends had proved their loyalty to me, my man proved his love, and I was living amongst a perfect peace.

So when I put on my newest swimsuit, I didn't think about gaining the approval of others. I was comfortable in my skin and knew my own approval was enough. One look in my full length mirror and I felt as cute as I always wanted to be. Of course the goal was to get better and better everyday, but at least I was on my way!

I was full of energy and feeling good. After a granola dipped in strawberry yogurt with a side of mixed nuts this morning, I was ready to embark on our sister's day out.

Music was blaring from my Bluetooth speaker so I moved swiftly to the beat as I readied myself to leave. That hot song we heard on our family vacation was playing on the radio. It reminded me of the tropical views and clear skies we had encountered. It brought me back to the good times before things had went bad.

"Hot like fiyah! Same creator make you!" It was a powerful statement. We all had our own bit of hotness to explore. I was finally finding mine in these curves and twists. "Dancing 'round mi yard. I have no regard! This here's my land and I always stand guard!"

In an instant, Daphne was in my room shaking her hips to the beat, singing right along with me. We were finally back where we used to be.

Family. Friends. Sisters. Forever.

"Girl, you ready?" she asked.

"Do I look ready?" I asked, exposing my figure from head to toe underneath my winter wrap.

"Sis, you stay ready. Let's go, gorgeous!"

"That means you've been rubbing off on me," I smiled. We both laughed as we head out my room door.

I was so feeling myself and feeling my family again too. All I needed was to let go and let love lead me.

As I walked outside into the brisk weather, I looked up into the clear sunny skies and whispered, "Thanks, mom."

She had given me the strength I needed to go on. Even without her physical presence, she had given me all the teachings I needed to win this war on low self esteem and hurt. Her love engulfed me and I would never let it go.

The End

PIECES OF MY SOUL
A Collection of Poems
By: Morgan Sawyer

Beauty

Beauty to me isn't judged by just what the eyes will see
Beauty is as beauty does, it's joy, peace, and positivity
Beauty isn't a color, a size, a name or price
It's not always a certain look and isn't always looked at twice

Beauty goes beyond a surface to the depths of ones soul
It's constant sense of giving is beauty's ultimate goal
Beauty isn't just portrayed on someone's fair skinned face
Nor is it determined by ones height, weight, or race

The media leads us to think there's just one set type to be
But truly we must know, it's simply beautiful to be free
Beauty is a state of mind, loving yourself and others
It's beautiful when you have support of fellow brothers

Beauty is knowing what makes you happy and why
Beauty is finding things in life that with strength, gets you by
Your smile is so beautiful, not because of straight, white teeth
For the joy it brings even when you're sinking down beneath

Finding good amongst bad is worth experiencing it all
The lesson you learned is beautiful and will guide your next fall
Beauty to me is an attitude, a persona and a mood
These things are all unchanging as true beauty never should

Most of what we believe is beauty will fade over time
We all know our grandfolks were once considered a dime
But even still, I see nana's beauty because I know her heart
She's had that peaceful spirit 'til the end from the very start

That's all I want to be, gorgeous from within
Attractive for my heart and grind, never for my skin
So when you so say I'm beautiful, I hope you truly see
The beauty I possess lies deep inside of me

Big and Bold

I remember the day like yesterday
It was way afterschool when I heard your voice vaguely
I knew those words would always protect me
A lone soldier had it seeming like the whole darn army
By the time we left, it was breezy out
My body was in pain but you brought me out
You showed me self love as simply as it should be
No drama, no fuss, you saw me for me
You let me in, gave me a comforted place
To rest my heart at a moderate pace
No confusion and no games when you're around
Just puppy love and peace as we make our rounds
Slowly but surely, you show me unconditional love
Big boy, curvy girl, a match made from above
Living mi vida loco, living yours on the boldest edge
We got a crazy bond, wrapped inside our heads
Always compared to siblings, this we wish to change
But we give all our love to fam, no time to feel estranged
All summer long had me missin' your attention
Dreamin' of your body, the passion, our connection
Knowing your heart, understanding the life you live
Tryna get you a message, knowing how hard it is to forgive
Life got real complicated for both you and me
But in my heart, mind, and soul you're still keepin' me
company
I pray this feeling lasts forever more
Because you will always be mi primer amor

Delicia B. Davis

Within the Skin

Don't be so quick to judge me by the skin I'm in
'Cause I'm not judging you, I want to know what is within
See, I don't care what it is that you expect from me
Because I don't fit your stereotypes, I'm all that I can be

See, within my skin, there is no hate, no animosity
No ignorance, let's clear the slate, but here's a bit of curiosity
Why are we still judged by the length our eyes will go?
Let's open up our minds, let's not be afraid to grow

Because our hands were meant to give, our hearts meant to love
But you only know that secret when your joy comes from the Man above
I want so badly for all people to grasp that simple concept
So that we all can live in peace the way Dr. King dreamt

Can we look beyond the surface? See past each other's eyes?
Because we all want justice served, but we need each other for each to rise

My granny has lots of stories of all the horrible things she saw
Most of which were caused by those darn Jim Crow laws
Rooted from a racism that a blind eye couldn't see
Growing through our people but I won't let that disease catch me
Let's all begin to see past the prejudice, look beyond the hate
I know it's all around us, but we don't have to live with that mind state

Because within the skin you'll find there's so much more than race
Behind our brown eyes, you'll find beauty past just the face
Within the skin, you may find love, a soft & warm gentle heart
If you've never looked within the skin, now's a great time to start

Who Am I?

While you're over there looking at me
Look into my eyes, what you see?
You see my dark eyes and my brown skin
But can you see the me within?

You see my clothes, my hairstyle too
Did you know I have something to say to you?
While you look on my surface and fail to see
The fascinating things I hold inside of me

The love I have for enemies and friends
Will go on loving, it has no end
I cannot change whatever pain I have caused
But get better and put negative things on pause

My family I appreciate but I guess not enough
There are just some times when they make it real tough
I fight and struggle keeping up with my school grades
While others think I have it all made

All my life, I have only wanted to succeed
To keep up in the world but it's difficult indeed
I fail and stumble, I digress and I fall
But people often forget, I cannot do it all

We all mistakes but not all can forgive
I realized that, in this life that I've lived
But I do my part, tryna make things right
Share my greatest gifts, because that's actually worth a fight

I may have loads of pain buried deep inside
They're buried down below 'cause those thoughts have died
Still moving on up, I'll reach the top
To progress as a person, I'll never stop

So look at me a little deeper, as deep as you can go
There's so much more I'd like for you to know
I've been misjudged and mistreated so many times
Next time, look a little deeper, read between my lines

 *Exotic*

(Lyrics)

So exotic, hypnotic; How I come around & touch your body
Smooth, like a rouge, and you'll never find another like me
I'm a tease, always please; come inside, you'll never leave
You good, in any hood; fly high above the woods
Foreign, imported; like nothin' afforded
From Jam rock to dis block; you love the way my body rock
Side to side, I dip it real low; I spin these hips so nice & slow
I'll show you culture, I won't divulge ya
Don't you be scared of this here departure
I purr like a cat, yea I talk that sweet smack
Don't ever lose me, you gon' want me back
Exotic like snake, watch the moves I make
Twisted, unlisted, stand back or escape
Curves like a leaf, aroma like a rose
got everything you want, and that's why you choose- meh!

Chorus

Exotic like a stranga , likkle hint a danga
Hot like fire, same creata make yuh!
Perfect like a sculpture, you nuh know Mi wah yuh
Show mi wha yuh got now, show me sup'm hot yah
Exotic like a flava, tasty like you savor
Something so delightful, love it like yuh savior
Soothing like a dream, you know what mi mean
We stay winning gold an mi need you pon di team

Let's go for a ride now, show me all your pride yow!
We own the land and we never gon' tun down
Hold up your flag, the crew got the bag
We feeling so fly, and I don't mean fi brag
I got the moves, yes, I get you loose, yes
We makin' black magic, yea, we light up the room
Open your eyes now, see what's around cha
This here's a banger and I know that you know that
♪ Love the skin I'm in, True beauty within
One hint of passion, a touch of your skin
Surrounded by hotness, inside and out
To my left, to my right, straight Up and about

Take me back to this, That's where my heart is
Home sweet home is where I find bliss
Dancing round mi yard, I have no regard
This here's my land (and) I always stand guard

Chorus ♪♪

Exotic like a stranga, likkle hint of danga
Hot like fiyah! same creator mek yuh
Perfect like a sculpture, you nah know mi wan yuh
Show me what you got now, show me sometin' hot yah
Exotic like a flavor, tasty like you savor
Sometin' so delightful, love it like your savior
Soothing like a dream, you know what mi mean
We stay winning (the) gold and mi need you pon di team

Bridge ♪♪

All different shades, I got it made
All so exotic, Can barely say names
Living in luxury, living so large
In every skin, you gotta go hard
Taste all this honey, it's dipped with rose gold
When God was makin me, he was breaking the mold
He wrapped me up in royalty, sealed me with love
Gave me millions of kisses from the sun up above

Download the hit song, "Exotic" for FREE at **deliciadavis.com**

Or check it out on **youtube.com**

Start Your Own Diary Now...

Dear Diary,

I am (name) _____ a
(relationship status, sexual orientation, gender)
_____.
I have (siblings, children, & pets) _____
_____.
I love (significant other[s], family member[s])
_____
_____.
I am usually feeling _____.
Today specifically, I am feeling _____.
I enjoy (hobbies, pastimes) _____.
What hurts me most is _____.
What angers me most is _____.
When I feel this, I _____.
When I need company, comfort, and support, I call on
(friends) _____.
I love to go (favorite places) _____.
I'm most afraid of _____.
I look forward to _____.
I aspire to _____.
I plan to change _____.
I like guys/girls who _____.
I'm feeling myself for 3 main reasons (3 things):
_____ _____ _____
I also want you to know, (share an intimate story,
feeling, moment, or issue) _____
_____.

To Continue writing, Purchase a "Dear
Diary", journal at DeliciaDavis.com
Do You have a juicy story to tell us all?
Share it at DiaryDiscussions.com

Dear Diary Word Search

Character's Names

```
T U J N B I F B P O J M D M L
I I W A V J V W N H A I T O E
N K F E N H P A D H E Y R R U
Q Y Y F F A H D A S M K E G N
R G L F A N T R E M Y E Y A A
Q E W E S N G L A T R O Y N M
Y O G J V R Y T Q A W F T D J
X D A N D E W S O I P O T F P
A Y H I A H C O C C Q L Y Z T
T K E N D R I C K I H N V W Z
D X A T R E G X H R S J P M L
N J R Q X T H R W T E Z O F X
T S U G V H W Y M A M Q D I S
V H D X R Q V V B P F W P Q D
Y D N I C S S I M P F L W A E
```

DAPHNE
DIESEL
DR. GRAHAM
EVELYN
JANA
JAY
KENDRICK
MANUEL
MISS CINDY
MORGAN
MR. GRANGER
PATRICIA
TAMMY
TIFFANY
TREY
TROY

About the Author

Delicia B. Davis is a Certified Health Educator and the award-winning author and publisher of the 'Dear Diary' young adult book series that focuses on social emotional and mental health issues existing in the lives of today's youth. She serves as the Director of a not-for-profit organization for the creative and social development of youth *Dream Team Leaders Inc.*, Founder of the performing arts company, *Dream Discovery Studios*, and contributor of the popular parenting magazine, *Mommy Noire*. Davis received her Bachelor's Degree (BA) in Media Studies and Journalism, is Mental Health First Aid certified in Youth and Adult care, and has received her Masters of Science in Education (MS.ed). She has gained resourceful experience in the business of arts & education having worked for BET News, Liberty Studios, Cox Enterprises, NYC Parks & Recreation, and currently as a Health Teacher with the NYC Department of Education. Her writing, public speaking, and performance skills are evident in all her works.

Delicia has appeared on *the Dr. Oz show*, ABC's *Good Morning America*, and *NY1 News*, amongst others. She has been publicly recognized for outstanding leadership, community service, production, and performance by numerous media outlets and esteemed leaders including NYS Senator **Leroy Comrie**, former Attorney General **Letitia James**, Councilman **I. Daneek Miller**, the *Queens Ledger Newspaper*, and the *Harlem Book Fair*, as a 2015 Finalist in their Phyllis Wheatley Book Awards. As a mother, friend, and inspirational woman, she lives by the words of wisdom she offers as an author & educator. Her mission is to share with the world that success is within reach and we all have the power to achieve it.

Meet the Author at one of
many book tour dates listed
at **DeliciaDavis.com**

Receive your **free** bookmark
jewelry with book purchase at
a live event!

Book the Author for public
speaking engagements, special
events, performances, & **free**
youth arts workshops!

www.ingramcontent.com/pod-product-compliance
Lightning Source LLC
Chambersburg PA
CBHW030520020726
47494CB00004B/1176